ANTON YORK, IMMORTAL

ALSO BY EANDO BINDER

Adam Link, Robot
The Double Man
The Eando Binder MEGAPACK®
Enslaved Brains
The Forgotten Colony
The Impossible World
The Mind from Outer Space

THE SAUCER SERIES

Menace of the Saucers
Night of the Saucers

ANTON YORK, IMMORTAL

EANDO BINDER

WILDSIDE PRESS

CONTENTS

CONQUEST OF LIFE

Chapter 1

The latter half of the 19th Century was a period of scientific giants—Ramsay, Bequerel, Roentgen, Einstein and others—but history does not mention Matthew York.

While the chemists outdid nature with synthetic products, while the physicists toyed with the amazing electron and the mathematicians groped into eternal secrets of the cosmos, Matthew York searched for a great scientific arcanum.

A brain highly stimulated by chronic hyperthyroidism pushed his investigations ahead in leaps and bounds, but it also burned him out before his time. Long years of intensive search and labor eventually crystallized into results.

Like a pilgrim who at last nears his Mecca, Matthew York knew, at the end, that his fingertips were at the door beyond which lay the secret. He knew at the same time, with resigned bitterness, that he would not live to open the door more than a crack.

"Give me ten more years!" he moaned to the Universe at large. "Ten paltry years, and I will give you back a thousand!"

But that was not to be, and Matthew York, like Columbus, was to die unknowing that he had reached the shores of a new land, though he had seen them in the distance.

* * * *

At twenty-five, Anton York, the son of Matthew York, was tall, physically perfect, mentally alert, with a budding scientific career already launched. At thirty he was healthier, if possible, and deep in the intricacies of electromagnetic waves applied to destruction. He sought a weapon so deadly that its use would teach the utter futility of war.

For Anton York had been in the World War. His grim experiences in that inferno of hate had left festering scars on his sensitive mind. He searched with all the passion of a fanatic for a Jovian weapon that would either end civilization or bring it everlasting peace.

Gradually it became apparent to him that he must be singularly blessed with physical good health. At times he wondered vaguely about it. It was hardly natural. Long hours in the laboratory, weeks of intensive, mind-shattering labor failed to weaken his superb vitality.

At thirty-five he reached his prime, with not a day's sickness behind him since childhood. It was as though some diligent guardian angel kept him free of the diseases that exacted their toll of all others around him. His researches had resulted in the development of a fused beam of ultrasound and gamma-rays—the long-sought goal.

Yet he did not reveal his discovery. It was too destructive, too likely to bring about chaos. He shelved it in utter secrecy, destroyed all recorded data, kept only the key formula in his mind for future use.

In conjunction with this ultra-weapon he also developed a super-refractive alloy which he patented for a small fortune. Thereafter he did not have the annoyance of financial insufficiency to hinder his personal researches. He abandoned the academic duties that had previously earned him a livelihood, and settled himself in his own laboratory.

At forty-five he had not aged at all, it seemed. He married a young and beautiful girl of twenty-five, one who instinct told him would not hold him back in his scientific endeavors. They looked like a well matched couple of equal age, for York seemed possessed of that elastic youthfulness with which some people are so fortunately endowed. Yet at times he caught himself wondering whether it was fortune or something else.

Ten years of research on liquid and solid rocket fuels had convinced him space travel would not be achieved by that clumsy, wasteful means. The answer, if answer there was to be, lay in solving the secret of gravitation.

At fifty-five he had made some steps, purely theoretical, toward the solution, but realized it might take several lifetimes to reach the fundamental basis necessary for an enduring analysis. He was like Anaxagoras, who had conceived an atomic theory, two thousand years before mankind had had a science capable of testing it.

"Vera," he said to his wife one day as she brought sandwiches to him in his experimental laboratory, "gravitation is like a planetary hypnotism, just as amazingly effective, and just as intangible. Just what it is I haven't yet determined, not even in theory. As far as I've gone, it seems to be a directive field of attraction between masses of matter. By directive, I mean radiating from points, rather than just filling space haphazardly, like the cosmic rays. Now there's a strong clue—"

Vera interrupted him. "Yes, dear, but drink your coffee before it gets cold."

"Vera, that clue is a will-o'-the-wisp I've been chasing down for ten years without success," he persisted. "It is very likely to take ten more tens of years. If only I had another lifetime ahead of me!"

"To look at you, you have." His wife was not merely flattering him. Her voice was serious, vaguely troubled. "I'm just thirty-five, and that's the age you look, yet you are fifty-five."

"I know, I know," murmured York, without elation.

"If it keeps up," Vera's voice wavered, "I'll be looking older than you in a few more years. Everybody comments on your youth, dear. They even call you a Dorian Grey—only in looks, of course, not character. Why, Tony, what—" York had dropped his sandwich, fingers nerveless. His face was pale.

"If it keeps up!" he cried, repeating his wife's phrase. *"If it keeps up!"*

"Tony, I don't understand."

"Neither do I," York told her earnestly. "Vera, I haven't spoken much about my childhood, but there's one thing that has haunted my subconscious mind like a vivid dream—the night when my father inoculated me with a solution that made me very ill for a month. It was a glowing liquid, that solution, as if a diamond had been dissolved in it. He called it an Elixir."

York's eyes grew misty with past memories.

"My father was a great scientist, greater than the world ever knew. He set himself a goal—the secret of life. He did strange things with mice and fruit flies, with his serum. Once he dipped some inoculated mice into a bath of deadly germ-laden fluid. The creatures lived on, undiseased."

He sprang up.

"In the name of God, what did his serum do to me? Why should I alone be free of disease? Why do I look like thirty-five at the age of fifty-five? What does it mean? I must find out!"

"Find out, but how?" ventured his wife. She was always awed by her husband's immunity to disease and senility, but she had trained herself to ignore the subject.

"From my father's diary, perhaps, or from his research notes. My aunt still has his papers. I've neglected to make a careful study of his notes. Now I'm going to make a thorough search for some clue to the mystery!"

Chapter 2

But it was not just a clue that York found as he meticulously examined Matthew York's voluminous data. It was the keystone of his quest itself. The entry in his father's diary for the day Anton York remembered so vividly, read in part:

Although it was against my better judgment, some madness seized me this night, and I injected 10 c.c. of a 50% water solution of the Elixir (leaf 88 A, book G-4) into Tony's left arm. I don't know what the result will be. God! I just don't know. No use to curse myself any more. It's done and only the future can give answer. In about six months, blood tests of Anton will indicate to what extent the Elixir has taken effect. Its cruder form, when it didn't kill my guinea-pigs, gave the sign of total disease resistance within that period. So in a half year Tony will either carry blood of high radiogenic capacity, or he will be dead. Dear God, not the latter! One thing I cannot get out of my mind is that my Elixir has connections with longevity.

Number 277-B-3 of my guinea-pigs, after inoculation, lived twice the normal span of life. And that was with the crude C-4 Elixir. Is it possible that in protecting protoplasm from disease by increased energy of radiogens in the body, the Elixir also prevents the decay of vitality? Preserves youth perhaps? If so, what will my Elixir M-7, just perfected, do to my Tony? Increase his life span, perhaps, to—no, I won't speculate. I am a scientist, not a prophet. Yet there must be some factor of longevity in the Elixir.

Longevity!

That word burst like a bomb in Anton York's brain. But he refused to allow his thoughts to carry on a train of speculation. Instead he searched out the "leaf 88A, book G-4" mentioned. Crabbed chemical formulae gave a compound labeled: "Grignard Reaction on the chlorinated union of zymase and pituitrin—in Elixir M-7."

Though not acquainted with the more technical phases of organic chemistry, being a physicist, York knew that zymase was an enzyme, a substance which could regenerate itself in the proper environment, though not a living material. A short search in his library gave him an idea of the properties of pituitrin. It was a gland product, controlling growth, keeping it even with the constant tearing down of protoplasm.

Growth and regeneration. Matthew York's formulae seemed to have combined these two biological factors. York puzzled over these for a while, then turned again to his father's diary. There was only one other entry after the one he had read. A month had been left blank. That was the month Anton York had been so ill from the injection. On the eve before his sudden death from heart failure, Matthew York had written:

Little Tony, thank God, is out of danger now. He is resting well, poor boy. I made a blood test today. Nothing definite. There is some slight increase of the radiogen value, though. I have just had the thought today that the longevity factor may be due to—simply—increased cosmic ray consumption. One of the unproven corollaries of the Radiogen Theory is that those invisible bundles of energy derive their power from the cosmic rays which fill every part of the Universe—every nook and corner of it, even the spaces between atoms. It is so astonishingly logical when one thinks of it. The countless radiogens which exist in and motivate protoplasm—give it "life"—are known to carry within their nuclei temperatures comparable to those of the stars, up to 6,000 degrees centigrade.

Cosmic rays, in turn, are electromagnetic waves of tremendous power and penetration. It is not fantastic to conceive of these constant rays losing their immense power to the radiogens, which are web-traps, like electromagnets. Now if resistance to disease—and I have almost proved it so—is the electrocution of germs by radiogens which they touch, an increased radio gen-content is a panacea. It has worked with certain of my guinea-pigs, mice and fruit flies. Pray God it works with Tony. Secondly, if old age is the waning capacity to manufacture radiogens, my Elixir is a drop from the Fountain of Youth, because its constituents are able to procreate themselves in protoplasm indefinitely.

And of course, there are my Methuselah fruit flies. A month ago, after inoculating Tony, I segregated those ten insects, gave them the same Elixir M-7, by inhalation, and they are still living, even though I did not feed them.

Normal fruit flies do not live more than fourteen days without food. Still I will not speculate in the case of Tony, except to say that if his radiogen-content is more than twice normal, he may well be—immortal! That is simply adding two and two to make four. I looked long at my boy today, wondering. He doesn't look any different, nor should he. But he may be—yes, I dare to think it—immortal!

Immortal!

If his radiogen-content was two times normal, he was incapable of dying either from disease or old age, both of which were results of deficiency of radiogens, according to the theory Matthew York had followed. Was this why he failed to grow old?

Examination of various other portions of his father's notes began to convince him it was. For the elder York had specified several times that an organism rich in radiogens, and capable of keeping up the abnormal supply, would reach its prime of life and stay there.

Gradually it became clear to Anton York as he read on. Living matter was a complete chemical entity in itself. Its "soul," or "life," came from the ultra-microscopic radiogens, like tiny batteries, which activated it under control of neuroimpulses from the brain.

The energy of the radiogens came from space, from the stars. When the Universe had been young, there had been more cosmic radiation, from the birth-throes of stars. Nature, with such a lavish supply of life-energy, had created a wide variety of life, but each with only enough radiogen-content to animate it properly. With the waning of the Universe, and the decline of cosmic radiation, Nature had increased the radiogen-content in inverse proportion in order to continue its original cycles of life.

But here was Man stepping in. Here was Matthew York defying Nature, outrunning Evolution. Here was Anton York with a twice normal capacity of utilizing the life-giving cosmic radiation.

Here was immortality! Because, not until the Universe had run down to half its present rate of cosmic radiation would Anton York be included in Nature's immutable laws of the cycles of life.

And that would not be for millions of years!

York grew dizzy with the thought of it.

"Bah!" he said suddenly, to himself. "Here I am talking myself into this thing without proof of any sort. I can't be sure that I have more radiogens than normal. I can't know that the Elixir worked on me. I can't even be sure that he succeeded as he hoped with his serum, for he wasn't absolutely certain himself."

This line of thought eventually led him to visit a famous blood specialist for a test. With a throbbing heart he waited to hear the result. The doctor finally reported that his blood was quite normal except in one respect—it had a singularly great germ-killing power. Twice as much as normal. He assured York that he would never be ill if his blood stayed that healthy.

York's eyes glowed like ingots of molten metal.

"Then that means my radiogen-content *is* doubled!"

The doctor frowned, then laughed.

"Oh, you mean according to the electromagnetic theory of life? That theory isn't credited, you know. In the accepted parlance, your blood simply contains twice as many phagocytes, the germ-killers. Radiogens make nice, scientific talk, but don't exist. If they did, life would be a matter of volts and amperes. We would have electrically rejuvenated people walking around and living forever." The doctor laughed heartily. "Think of that."

A sort of paralyzing calm came over York, along with the conviction that the doctor was wrong, and his father right. A voice seemed to beat in his brain, telling him that his suspected immortality was not altogether mythical.

"How old am I?" he questioned him.

The doctor looked him over, though surprised at the question.

"I'd say about thirty-two, not more than thirty-five."

"I'm fifty-five," stated York. "And a hundred years from now I'll still be looking thirty-five." He left the gaping doctor, went out into the street. He stared at a tall, sturdy skyscraper. "You're strong and enduring," he said to it quietly. "You'll last fifty, a hundred years. I'll outlast you and your successors." To the river under the steel bridge he murmured: "Some day you will not exist, and I will stand over your dried bed." To the fields he whispered: "You will nurture many, many crop cycles, but some day you will be barren. On that day—I will be thirty-five."

Night came and to the bright stars he hurled a challenge: "The eternal stars, eh?"

Hours later, in a rosy dawn, he came to himself. He found himself far out in the country, and realized he had been walking in a daze, drunk with the thought of immortality. Vera was waiting for him when he arrived home, tired and muddy.

"Tony! I've been worrying."

York looked at her strangely. A thought struck him, one that had persisted before.

"Yes, I've been worrying too. One little worry stuck with me all during last night, even in the heights of my fancy. That thought is losing you." He pulled her to him suddenly, fiercely. The love he had for her was deep and vital.

"I love you madly," he cried, "but I'll lose you, unless—"

"Tony! What are you saying?" Vera's eyes became haunted with fear—fear for his sanity.

"No, dear, I'm all right," York said quietly. "I can't explain now, but soon I shall." His eyes shone then. "Soon you and I—together—"

Chapter 3

"Hmm, I don't know if I can duplicate it. The main part of the serum is not so intricate, but this one ingredient is new to organic chemistry. Look at it. If you know anything at all about my field you'll realize that combining zymase and pituitrin, a chlorinated enzyme and an acidic gland product, is impossible. I don't think it can be done."

The speaker was Dr. Charles Vinson, a skilled technician of the biochemical sciences. He and York had been acquainted academically twenty years before.

"You must duplicate that serum!" York's voice trembled with desperation. "I can't be as frank about this as I'd like, Dr. Vinson, but the manufacture of that serum means more to me right now than anything in the world.

Try it, anyway. Work here at my laboratory for a month, a year, and name your price."

"Oh, it is not the money," protested the biochemist. He did not quite mask the inherent cupidity of his nature, however. His eyes gleamed with sudden interest. "It would cost much. Your place here is equipped for electrons and volts, not bacteria and guinea-pigs. I would have to buy much—"

"Then it is agreed," declared York. "At any cost, make me 10 c.c. of this Elixir."

"Elixir!" Dr. Vinson's whole manner changed. "Elixir, did you say? Where did you copy these formulae? What do they represent?"

"Bluntly, none of your business." York could not hide a trace of anger. He had never particularly liked the biochemist. For a moment he was sorry he had picked him. Yet he knew it would be difficult to find a more capable man for the task.

Dr. Vinson shrugged. York went on: "You will be paid for duplication of the serum, nothing more. Look over this chemical annex to my laboratories. Whenever you are ready, come to the library. I'll discuss terms and procedure with you." He wheeled about and left.

Dr. Vinson studied the sheet in his hand. It was a typewritten copy of someone's research notes. Whose? What did they represent? An Elixir? Further pondering suddenly enlightened him. Matthew York—Anton York: father and son. Many years before Matthew York had published a short treatise on the secret of life. He had claimed that an electrical interpretation of life was the only approach to its mystery. He created a small furor, and his paper became the forerunner of radiogenic theory. Yet nothing more had been heard of Matthew York.

Except perhaps this. Dr. Vinson held up the sheet, wondering.

That same day York spoke to his wife eagerly. For the first time he explained to her fully the secret of his youth—the immortality of his flesh. She was not so surprised as she might have been. She caught her breath sharply, though, when he added: "And when Dr. Vinson makes up some of the serum, it will be for you! You and I will have each other forever in perpetual youth, in our prime of life!"

She was suddenly in his arms, sobbing.

"I will love you for all eternity!"

* * * *

In the next month York's laboratory became the receiving end of a small caravan of new materials. Varieties of chemicals, crates of apparatus, cages of squealing guinea-pigs. For Dr. Vinson had seen at a glance that the serum was not to be an elementary accomplishment.

In another month he had started to gain results. York came often to watch him work. He seldom spoke. His attitude was one of waiting, and impatiently. Sometimes his wife was with him, and they would watch together, smiling at one another secretly.

Vinson did not give up trying to draw out York in conversation about this mysterious project.

"York," he complained one day, "there's something missing in the data I'm working on. I'll have to have it all. Where are the original notes?"

"Why do you need them?" York countered hesitantly.

"Because something I need may be in them. Some little thing you neglected to copy, but vital to successful duplication. Look at this guinea-pig. The serum killed him, as it has all others, because it is not the right serum."

York faltered. Some instinct had kept him from showing his father's notes up until now, for they dealt with a tremendous thing. Yet he wanted the serum. And because the Infinite did not warn him, he yielded. But only the scientific notes, not the diary.

Dr. Vinson's over-eager hands leaped the yellowed pages. His eyes glittered first, then narrowed. A pattern was piecing itself together in his mind.

Not many weeks later the biochemist's face was bright with triumph. Together with York he watched the healthy antics of a guinea-pig into whose veins the day before had been injected an overdose of bubonic plague germs.

"That little animal is germ-proof!" announced Vinson excitedly. "It has passed the last test. It is immune to any but violent death. We have the same serum now that your father developed."

York turned swiftly.

"My father! How did you know? What—"

The biologist smiled thinly.

"Why beat around the bush, York? Your father developed this serum and tried it on you. It was dangerous, because the serum was fatal half the time. Yet he took the chance, knowing that if you survived, you would be immune to disease." His face changed subtly. "And immortal!"

"Damn you!" cursed York, stepping forward.

"Wait, York. I haven't been spying around. The thing stared me in the face. You, who should be as old as I am, fifty-five, look like thirty-five. Then, I can show you a fruit fly that has lived twice its normal span and will continue to live—who knows—through all eternity. It astounded me until I reasoned it out."

York relaxed. After all, it was too tremendous a secret to conceal from the man who had worked with his father's notes. He stared at the biochemist uncertainly. What would this mean?

Dr. Vinson laughed shortly.

"You are an immortal, York. And you love your wife. You want her by your side in the long future that beckons. Hence, my work here—to manufacture the Elixir, for her. Well, let me warn you—there is an even chance that your wife will not gain immortality, but death!"

"I'm going to take the chance," York said. "Prepare a suitable dose for injection. In case of death—"

He made a resigned gesture. "Vinson," he continued, solemnly, "you and I share a great secret. The Fountain of Youth! An age-old dream come true. After my wife has been inoculated, we'll have to discuss—many things. This Elixir can be a great gift to civilization, to mankind. In my own case it will allow me to finish my researches, to solve the secret of gravitation, which I could not do in one lifetime. But certain problems would arise if the Elixir were given to the world. You can guess them."

Vinson did not answer. His small eyes blazed with the dawning gleam of some staggering idea. York noticed the sudden stiffening of his body, spoke sharply.

"Well?" It was a challenge.

The biochemist's dry lips parted but no sound came. Then with an effort he gasped: "Death! If your wife dies, think of the responsibility, the guilt!"

If York had not been so preoccupied with his own problems, he would have demanded the truth. For Vinson had not spoken what was crawling in his mind—something of far greater significance than the mere fate of one woman.

"The responsibility is all mine," snapped York. "I have her full consent to this. We have also made out a legal document absolving me from all blame in case of her death under the serum. According to law, this is not contestable in court any more, so long as the parties concerned are mentally sound. You are not an accessory to a crime in any sense, for there is no crime. When can you have the stuff ready?"

"In about three days," answered Vinson, voice curiously hushed. His face looked fevered; his hand trembled. "You see, I want to do my best with the serum for your wife. Purify it as much as possible. Increase the odds in our favor."

York put a hand to the biochemist's shoulder.

"Come, don't take it so hard," he said, vaguely aware that the man was more than normally moved.

Vinson smiled weakly. York left, to tell Vera of the near approach of the great moment when they would look down the interminable hall of the future together. When the door had closed behind him, the biochemist's face gave way to pent-up emotions he no longer had to hide. A twisted smile came over the thin lips that hissed, "Fool!" in the direction of the vanished York.

If there is some repetitious twist to the workings of fate, certainly it became manifest in the events that occurred three nights later. For in broad detail it was the ancient story of eternal love, of Romeo and Juliet, re-enacted.

Tall, handsome, physically perfect, Anton York stood over the body of his wife, his face marked with grief. She lay on a couch, her beautiful face molded in the peaceful lines of death. Dr. Vinson stood to one side, like a dumfounded Belthasar, breathing hard. He stared mutely from the hypodermic in his hand to the pair before him.

Just a few minutes before, with York holding his wife's hand, he had injected the serum into her arm. The reaction had been sudden and startling. Her breathing had grown hard, her eyes had flown wide. With a little half sob and half smile to her husband, she had fallen back on the couch.

Then a few racking gasps, after which an ominous stillness had come over her relaxed form.

Vinson dropped the hypodermic and stepped beside the couch. He leaned over to listen for heart beats. Then he looked up.

"Dead!" he whispered huskily. "The odds were not quite even, for her!"

York's face was a blur of overwhelming, repressed despair. Though Vinson had repeatedly warned him that this could be the result, he had not been prepared for it. He dashed from the room suddenly, without a word.

Alone with the body, Vinson stared at the sweet face somewhat fearfully. It shook his resolve to try the Elixir himself, which was necessary for the furtherance of certain plans he had made. Immortality or death! Was it worth the risk?

York suddenly burst into the room, face pale and desperate. Ignoring the biochemist, he dropped to his knees beside the couch. For a long moment he gazed at the face so dear to him. Then, with a swift motion he brought one hand up toward his mouth. Vinson caught the glint of glass, uttered a strangled cry.

But it was already done. York gave him a wan smile.

"Cyanide," he whispered. "That is a better Elixir for eternal life." A minute later he slumped across the body of his wife, pale blue around the lips.

Dr. Vinson gaped at the double tragedy. For a moment he was weak with horror of death. But presently he straightened up, smiled.

"Perhaps it is better this way," he mused. "York might have resisted my plans. He is—was—the altruistic sort. He would not have approved, I'm sure. And I had determined anyway that nothing was to stand in my way."

He laughed shortly. "The fool! With the greatest gift mankind ever had in his hand, he thought only of making his wife immortal. I suppose later he would have envisioned centuries of research for himself—to benefit mankind. He could not think of the important thing—power! The power of immortality! But I think of it. Yes. First, I'll purify the Elixir further—give myself a greater chance to survive it. Then—"

He broke from a trance, whirled about.

"Got to get out," he told himself. "I must not be connected with this affair. I must be left alone—to think, to plan, to build." He rolled the phrase on his tongue, eyes gleaming with a fanatic fire. "I'll change my name. Get all my money together and leave the country perhaps. Build in secret. This marks a new phase in my life, and in the history of the world!"

He turned once more to the still forms on the couch. With the sense of melodrama still upon him, he whispered: "We shall either meet again soon, in eternal death, or never in an eternity!"

Chapter 4

Dr. Vinson left and made his way to the laboratory in which he had duplicated the Elixir. Here he heaped all of Matthew York's notes on the floor, set fire to them. In his brain was locked the great secret of the serum. On sudden thought he took a gallon jar of alcohol and rolled it toward the burning papers. He watched until the heat cracked the glass and sprayed liquid fire over the floor. The flames licked at the wooden workbenches, grew to a vigorous blaze.

Vinson turned away with a dark smile shadowing his face.

"From these ashes will spring my immortal empire!" he cried aloud. Then he left the place.

The eager flames became a yellow holocaust in the big building that housed the laboratory and home of Anton York. But fate had not played out its re-enactment of history's Romeo and Juliet. In the room where a double tragedy had seemed to occur, there was a stir of life.

Vera opened her eyes and struggled to sit up on the couch. Her husband's body slid away, fell to the floor gently. Her horrified eyes saw this and with a scream of terror she fell back again, pale as death.

But it was not the dagger-death of Juliet. She had only fainted. When York opened his eyes a moment later, his mind was an aching blank. A rush of memory brought him to his feet with a groan. He stood there a moment, trying to fathom his escape from death. He could not know that the same super-electrical quality of his flesh which resisted disease and supplied the energy of youth was also able to fight the fatal fire of life-poisons with its own youth-fires.

A thick cry of unbelief escaped him as he saw that his wife was breathing. There were two fevered spots of red on her marble cheeks. Death had passed them both by! Again it was an enigma to him that the powerful serum, producing a temporary coma, like that before death, had finally eased its stricture of the heart and lungs and allowed life to continue in her body.

A curl of smoke under the door warned York of the danger. He swung it open and as quickly closed it as a cloud of smoke swept into the room. He picked up his wife in strong arms and ran from the building. There was a faint dismay in his heart over the loss of the laboratory, but a far greater joy that they were alive. And alive as immortals, both of them!

A month later, in a hospital, York's tired eyes lit up happily.

"The danger is over, Vera," he told her. "You went through the same period of illness that I did when my father gave me the serum as a child. It's like the fevers that follow vaccination. But it's over now, and you and I together can look down the centuries!"

Three months after this, in a hotel, Vera asked about Vinson.

"Dr. Vinson disappeared in the fire," York told his wife, "and I'm worried about him. I can't rest until I know where he is. He alone has my father's secret—the original notes were destroyed together with all copies. What is he doing with the Elixir? I can't help feeling concerned, because he is not the man to use such a thing wisely."

* * * *

A year later, he said resignedly: "I guess there's no use to hunt him further. I've employed the most expert detectives, but they've found no trace. Wherever Vinson has gone, he's covered his trail completely. And that's ominous. Again, he may have tried the serum and died from it. I wish I could hope that."

Two years later, York proudly surveyed his new laboratories, located in a remote part of the mountains. It was made possible by one of his inventions. A large industrial concern had patented his super-magnet, a by-product of his previous researches in gravitational phenomena.

"Here," he predicted, "I shall solve the secret of gravitation."

Five years later he had come to the conclusion that gravitation exhibited lines of force, much like a magnet. "What is wrong with the analogy of converting kinetic motion into electricity by cutting the lines of magnetic force?" he asked himself. "If the field of gravitational force is similarly cut—yes, but with what?"

Ten years later, he frowned at a new snag in his researches.

Ten years after that, with careful planning, he and Vera changed their names, to circumvent explaining their permanent youth.

A decade later they had achieved a harmony of continued existence, and mortality seemed a dream in their past.

Time swept by. Its rolling pace did not change the couple in their mountain laboratory-home. They were still thirty-five in appearance and vigor. They lived in a state of detachment from the rest of the world. From the sidelines, they watched the kaleidoscopic march of events, the unfurling of history. Strikes, famines, elections, social changes, shifting national boundaries, new inventions—their televisor kept them informed.

York's experiments took him into a field wholly untouched—the phenomena of the gravitational lines of force. A field as untouched as the electromagnetic scale before Newton and his successors explored it. It had taken over two centuries, and a host of diligent savants, to understand radio waves and cosmic radiation, the limits of that field. York labored to explore his field alone, and in less than two centuries.

In a way, York was equal to a line of scientists following one goal. Each time he reached some hiatus and had to branch away. He was like a new worker taking up the work another had left in death. And he had the advantage of always being in perfect condition, physically and mentally.

Thus it was, that a task that normally would have required all of a thousand years of science fell before his irresistible onslaught. He called his wife in excitedly one day.

"I've cut the force-lines of gravitation," he said triumphantly. "I use light-beams, curved ones, for the energy source. I feed them into the quartz coils, like electricity in a helix of copper wire, to create a magnetic field. A magnetic field is used in opposition to another magnetic field to produce kinetic motion. My quartz field produces a gravitational field, in opposition to Earth's gravity, to produce kinetic motion. Unlimited kinetic motion—direct from Earth's gravitational field!"

York's voice became a paean of enthusiasm.

"It is the answer to space travel, if I can refine my apparatus to the point where a single beam of direct sunlight will actuate my quartz rotors. I must also make a sun-charging battery to spin the rotors, so that a ship in space will need only the perpetual sunlight to motivate it. Vera, I am close!"

Close, yet it took another quarter century to achieve it. It was almost a hundred after the inoculation of Vera that York gave his ship its first tryout. It was a ten-foot globe of light metal, set with several thick quartz port-windows. Two large convex mirrors at the top were arranged to feed sunlight to knobs of sensitive selenium. Some miracle of York's science compelled the sun's radiant energy to pour into the ship like water into a funnel.

It handled awkwardly at first, until York got the feel of changing his artificial gravity fields. Then he was able to whisk the heavy globular ship about with flashing speed. It looked like a bright steel bomb from some giant cannon.

He leaped out of its hatchway, panting, after landing.

"I can't tell you how excited I am over this," he told his wife. "Think of it. We can stock the ship with necessities and go out into space, explore the other planets!"

They made a trip to the moon and back that same year. From this experience York was able to refine his apparatus still more. They made a trip to Mars and to Venus. He began planning a trip to another star. This would require a larger ship for supplies and motors to be run by starlight and tenuous mid-void gravitational forces, and he began its construction. If his gift of immortality had made him feel like a god, this ability to explore the ether was still more of a god-given attribute.

He opened his eyes one day to realize he had been drunk with these things, as he had been with the first realization of immortality. Earnestly, then, he sat down to write out the complete plans for his anti-gravity unit. He would send this to every scientific institution of the world.

It was just before he had finished the long and complicated paper that Vera called his attention to startling news over the radio. All during the past year there had been mysterious invasions in outlying sections of the world. Mysterious, but unimportant in that they involved obscure regions. The invaders had always come in small, swift ships, equipped with incredibly destructive weapons. Many garbled reports had been received from places invaded, but no one seemed to know just who or what was responsible.

But this night, the news was alarming.

"Rome has just undergone a terrific bombing by a mysterious fleet of small, fast aircraft," an excited announcer told the world. "They may be the same ones that have been terrorizing Earth in the past year. All the world is aroused. What nation has done this cowardly thing, attacking without warning?"

York's eyes reflected again the emotions that had haunted him in the World War.

War! That most senseless of human atrocities.

"Haven't they had enough of it?" he cried. "They fought like beasts for a decade just thirty years ago. I was tempted then to reveal my super-weapon and let them butcher one another to nothingness. I am tempted now."

The next day Berlin was bombed. And in the following days, Paris, London, and Moscow. The world gasped. What mad nation was challenging all Europe? Tokyo was bombed, and then Washington. What power was challenging the whole world? A new note of terror arose when a gigantic fleet, composed of mixed Italian and German aircraft, was annihilated by fifty small ships of the invaders. The enemy seemed to have some long-range weapon that made victory ridiculously easy.

York waited for the unknown power to declare itself. Then he would act. After the succession of bombings, which had not been very destructive and had evidently been an exhibition of power, there was a lull of a day, then news that set the world on fire.

"The enemy had finally announced itself," blared the televisor. "This afternoon a powerful radio message was picked up at many official stations. The invaders that have bombed the world's most important cities call themselves The Immortals. They demand a parley of all important nations, at which The Immortals are to be accepted as the sole government on earth. In plain words, The Immortals, whoever they are, demand world dominion. This, or the threat of continuous bombing and destruction by their invincible fleet of fifty ships!"

Then York knew. He and Vera looked at one another. "Dr. Vinson!" gasped York. "Dr. Vinson and a band of ruthless demons bent on conquering Earth. For a hundred years he planned this. I did not think he would go to such lengths. In some hidden spot he and his crew, all immortals, must have labored for this day. Undoubtedly they are all scientists and technicians. Men who in a century's time could do miracles in discovery. Vastly improved ships, superweapons, carefully laid plans. They played for big stakes and made preparations in a big way."

He turned his anger on himself.

"Why didn't I see it before this? It's all so clear now. In the past year they carried out experimental raids, to gauge their power and readiness. I should have suspected, and prepared. Now they have struck, and the end will be soon. True scientific warfare against the world's tremendous, but clumsy armament. The wasp against the bear. It can sting again and again, too quick and small to be crushed by might."

Again news came over the televisor, indicating the crisis which faced the world. A hastily and secretly formed armada of the world's best fighting craft—of every large nation—had massed and challenged The Immortals. The challenge had been promptly accepted. The incredible story told by gasping announcers was that by sheer weight of numbers the fleet had succeeded in downing three of the enemy, while they themselves were mowed to one-third their strength. The remnant had fled.

Vera was alarmed by the sickly grey color of York's face as he heard this.

"I'm responsible," he whispered hoarsely. "I let the dangerous secret of immortality fall into Vinson's hands!" His whisper continued, but with a deadlier note in it: "I must act before it is too late."

It was the climax of his super-lifetime. Armed with nothing more than a few pages of diagrams and figures, York descended on Washington in his silent gravity ship and said he could fight the alien power. He was derided rather than laughed at, in that the situation was too grim for laughing.

Chapter 5

However, the gravity ship could not be laughed at. And when a group of scientists was hurriedly assembled, they said the thing looked good on paper. At the same time the startling news came that The Immortals had been completely victorious in Europe and were now sweeping Asia. If Japan would fall, as must be, America would be next, as the last remaining power.

Faster than they had ever moved before, the wheels of industry, lashed by a frantic government, turned out the apparatus York wanted. He had them secretly move their headquarters to Pittsburgh. The terrible weapon he had kept locked in his brain for over a century took form here.

In two weeks it was nearly completed, but not before The Immortals, now dominant in the Eastern Hemisphere, swung their tiny, deadly fleet westward. At the first encounter, the pride of America's aerial defense was annihilated by the sweeping rays of the enemy. These rays had all the potency of a two-ton bomb at close range, yet were invisible and noiseless.

"We must surrender!" This cry echoed in the hall of authority.

"Hold out!" commanded York. "Hold out, I tell you." They obeyed him, almost hypnotized by his blazing eyes. The Immortals, after defiance of their ultimatum, promptly began razing cities to the ground. Their supply of fuel and ammunition seemed inexhaustible. Coming from the west, San Francisco, Denver and St. Louis crumpled before the onslaught.

"Enough is enough. We must give in!" was the horrified clamor among the leaders and statesmen.

"Hold out!" screamed York. "Three more days!"

They did. In those three days Chicago, Cincinnati and Philadelphia became smoking ruins. And the invincible fleet headed for New York City!

But in those three days York became prepared. His weapon was mounted on his ship, a long snout of vitrolite pivoted on a universally jointed base. Wires led inside the ship, through hastily made rips in the hull, to the power source of the ship. By a quick change, York had fitted his antigravity unit to utilize Earth's tremendous gravitational field for power for the vitrolite gun.

Then he contacted the fleet of The Immortals by radio, challenged them, called them back from their course toward New York. They might have taken it as a desperate bluff to save that great city except that York made his challenge a personal one—from himself to Dr. Vinson.

"York?" came back a voice that was recognizable as Dr. Vinson's. "Anton York? Impossible—he—"

"I did not die, Vinson. I survived the cyanide. I've been wondering if you would appear on the scene. I'd almost forgotten you in the century that has gone by. But bad pennies always show up. You've done a lot of damage, Vinson, but you'll do no more. I'll meet your fleet anywhere you say for a showdown. If you don't meet me halfway, I'll hound you to the ends of the earth—to the ends of the Universe if I must!"

Vinson's voice spluttered over the radio. For the first time his companions around him saw fear on their leader's face. What man could this York be, that their hitherto confident master feared him?

Then Vinson spoke again: "Wait, York. I don't know what you have to give you such confidence against my fleet, but listen to reason. You're an Immortal, as we are. You belong with us, York—as rulers of Earth. I have no grudge against you. Join up with me and that's the end of it. Why should there be trouble between us?"

York's voice was a white-hot hiss in the microphone.

"You will rule Earth without me, or not at all. But first you must put me out of the way. Name the place!"

"Over Niagara Falls!" Vinson's voice, previously uncertain, rang now with arrogance and assurance "What can you do against the fleet that has whipped a world?"

It must have seemed like a battle of the gods to those fortunate eyes that saw it, especially those who had caught the exchange of words between York and Vinson.

York's ship, a bright ball of metal and glass, dropped from the clouds several miles from the fleet of The Immortals. A group of tiny black figures could be seen around the base of the vitrolite gun, precariously hung in sprung seats. These were the gunners, iron-nerved army men who knew nothing about the weapon, but who knew that when you aimed the long snout and jerked a lever, a something was released that could destroy. Other than that they had only grim determination and courage.

Like the buzzing of angry hornets, Vinson's fleet dashed for the lone ship. York's ship, high over Lake Erie, hovered like a poised eagle. The long, slender vitrolite tube swung toward the oncoming ships. Something blue and pulsating sprang from it, projected a streamer of violet across the intervening space of two miles.

What inconceivable force it was, no one was ever to know. York could have described it briefly as a combination of atom-tuned sound vibrations and electron-tuned gamma vibrations, both together able to rip matter to ultra-shreds, without revealing its secret. For it was a type of wave existing in the audio-ether transition stage between the known and the unknown in catalogued science.

But the effect was not so mysterious. A dozen of the enemy craft sagged strangely, burst into little bubbles of vapor, and changed to clouds of black dust that fell slowly toward the water below. The rest of the fleet, as one, swept up and to one side, away from this frightful weapon. Yet before they had completed the retreat, twelve more of their ships had become puff-balls of black soot.

York smiled grimly. He had purposely made the focus of the gun's beam very wide. Each time it belched forth its Titanic charge, a ransom in power went with it. But Earth could afford it, with its almost unlimited gravitational stresses that fed the weapon.

The range of The Immortals' weapons was known to be just as great, but they had not thought to use them on this lone ship three miles away. Now, however, the air droned with the concussion of atmospheric rents made by invisible streamers of their ray-forces. Their rays were amplified cathode radiations, million-watt bundles of electrons at half the speed of light.

York was not caught napping. His ship had already moved upward, at right angles to their position, presenting a target moving at a speed of ten thousand miles an hour. It was cruel for the men exposed to the air around the vitrolite gun, but necessary. York flung his ship above the clouds.

The Immortals seemed nonplussed. They scattered widely and massed their beams upward, on the blind chance of scoring a hit. When York's ship did appear, far on the other side of his former position, it was heralded by the destruction of eight more of Vinson's fleet. Most of his ships were already destroyed and the fight had hardly begun!

Under this scene, the waters of Lake Erie boiled and rose in great clouds of steam. Niagara Falls, though York tried to avoid it, took most of one of his gun's charges, and became in one minute an unrecognizable jumble of churning waters and puffs of black vapor. Grim reminder for all time of this battle of the gods.

The Immortals fled, ingloriously, scattering wide. The swift, sweeping sword of destruction from York's ship picked them off one by one. There was no limit to its range. It hounded the last one down after a brief chase. And the menace of the Immortals was over!

The world had to content itself with honoring three of the five men who had handled the vitrolite gun, and burying the other two, dead from their ordeal. York, after landing them, had promptly departed, without a word to anyone. Without waiting for thanks and praises. Like a god he had come and like a god he left.

And like a god he went out into the void not long afterward, with his wife, leaving behind him the legacy of space travel. The secret of the super-weapon went with him. The secret of immortality was no longer his to give away. Earth had had a god, one who had nearly destroyed it, and then saved it. One who had shown the way to other worlds. One who had exhibited an awesome weapon to warn mankind what its warfare could lead to. One about whom many legends were to be woven, true and false.

But now the god was gone—forever. Once given a taste of the supreme freedom of the void, he could not return to the pettiness of Earth. Nor did he care to interfere in any way, altruistic or otherwise, in its normal course of affairs.

On and on he went, he and his immortal companion. Their understanding and wisdom grew to cosmic heights.

They visited many worlds, many suns. Time meant nothing. They discovered the secret of voluntary suspended animation, requiring no food or air. They became truly gods.

Somewhere in the dim future ages he must die, this man-made god. Sometime when the scales of Time have sufficiently lowered the amount of cosmic radiation which gives the god life.

LIFE ETERNAL

Chapter 1

Mason Chard laughed.

For a year now he had been cruising aimlessly in the interplanetary depths of the Solar System. His beryllium-hulled space ship was motivated by the controlled interplay of the gravitational stresses filling the void. His power plant greedily absorbed solar radiation and rammed it through whirling quartz coils which cut the force-lines of gravitation, producing reactive motion. The same titanic energies which swung the ponderous planets in their eternal orbits were used, in part, to propel the tiny ship. It was super-power, limitless. And eternal, in the sense that gravitation was eternal.

Eternal!

Mason Chard liked that word. For, barring violent death, Mason Chard himself was eternal! In his veins flowed blood enriched with a self-renewing enzyme that was the antithesis of death and decay. His body cells were doubly endowed with radiogens, the tiny batteries of life which sucked energy from the cosmic rays, from the universe at large.

Mason Chard could not die from "disease" or "age" until the Universe had run down to the point where cosmic radiation was halved. That would be millions of years in the future!

The Immortal laughed again. His ruminations covered, in reverse order, the most eventful thousand years in human history. Just the year before, Earth's vigorous race had established an outpost on far Pluto, thus completing a phase in its empire building. Previous to that there had been interplanetary wars, heroic pioneering, and dauntless feats of exploration. The parade of a thousand years, glorious and packed with drama, marched through Mason Chard's mind. The laughs that punctuated his ponderings were for those times he, Chard, had interfered with the course of history.

There was the time, for instance, he had led the insurrection of the native Callistans against the domineering Earthmen, purely for the diversion of espousing a lost cause. At another time it had been his whim to destroy three successive rescue ships on their way to a marooned group of explorers in the wilds of Titan, so that he could watch brave men die.

Chard had had to amuse himself in those endless centuries to escape the dreary cycles of ennui. He had long felt himself above the ties of race and allegiance. Roaming the interplanetary void at will, a mysterious and half-mythical anarchist, he had often dammed the progress of mankind's growing dominion in the Solar System. Along with the ties of blood and tradition, Chard had thrown conscience into the discard. It had not caused him one twinge to see thousands of space ship crews annihilated in the intra-world war he had personally embroiled, five centimes before, between Venus and Earth. He had watched the holocaust through his vision screen, grimly amused.

Mason Chard had never taken the trouble to analyze himself. If he had, he would have realized himself to be a colossal ego, inflated by the drug of immortality. He would have recoiled from the picture of a cold, heartless, scheming scoundrel, clothed in a super-vanity. Yet perhaps only one little thing made him this, rather than an honored, inspired, immortal leader—

His chuckle was just a bit bitter as reminiscences took him back to that time almost a thousand years ago when he had run afoul of Earth law. Realizing his immortality, he had started an abortive drive for world domination. He had not planned thoroughly and had been captured. Fortunate that capital punishment, even for treason, was outlawed in that day, he had been exiled to a lonely asteroid. His sentence had been 199 years. There, for seventy-five years, he was made to attend the warning light beacon that warded off space liners. A supply ship had come once a year.

The only light spots in that dreary, bitter incarceration were those times the officials had been amazed at his longevity, not knowing he was immortal. He had been a man in the prime of life at the start of his sentence. He was still a man in the prime of life seventy-five years later. He might have waited to serve out his 199 year sentence, to confound them utterly, but before that a pirate of space landed to destroy the beacon in some deep-laid plot. Chard gratefully joined the pirate crew, became their leader in a few years, and later betrayed them.

Thus had his career begun. Then Chard's reflections went back to the stirring events of the middle Twentieth Century.

He had been thirty-five then—really thirty-five—occupied as a research scientist. Dr. Charles Vinson, his former instructor, had called him to a secret conference with a half hundred others, unfolding a breath-taking scheme. He had inoculated them all with the Elixir of Youth, whose formula he had stolen from Anton York, and as immortals they had begun the subjugation of Earth. Anton York himself had defeated the plan, destroying the Immortal fleet.

Of the Immortals, only Mason Chard was left. He had been left in charge of their secret underground headquarters in Tibet and had thus escaped York's vengeance. For years he had remained in hiding, waiting until Anton York had left the Solar System, plunging out amid the stars like a god whose duties were done. Chard, keeping his identity secret, had watched Earth, equipped with the legacy of space travel York had left, attempt the conquest of the Solar System.

And then had come his lone and foolish attempt to win the rule of Earth. Reaching again this point in his review of the past, Chard laughed once more, this time harshly.

"A thousand years I've fooled around and played with fate," he muttered to himself, staring out at the dome of stars. "But I have learned much. I am prepared now to accomplish the aim that Vinson tried and failed, and I later, and before us, men like Napoleon, Attila the Hun, and Alexander the Great. I am going to conquer the world. Not the world they knew, but the world of today—the entire Solar System!"

His cold, cruel eyes blazed with sudden fire.

"I have the power to do it. And more important, I know the method. It must be done through fear! Fear is the common weakness of all humanity, excepting myself. I have learned to laugh at fear. But these mortals, they know fear. It can strike them powerless, tie their hands and wits. I will conjure up a fear that will strike in every heart in the Solar System. I will play up this fear, feed it, until they grovel at my feet. I will become emperor of nine worlds!"

In the melodramatic ecstasy of the moment, Mason Chard flung a clenched fist toward the watching stars, pledging himself.

"One against six billions—and I will win!" he boasted. Once again his super-ego had found something on which to feed itself.

Chapter 2

Somewhere, far out in interstellar space, Anton York, a man-made god, roamed the uncharted deeps of the void. Immortal and wise beyond human understanding, he plunged on in a timeless lethargy, taking pleasure in observing the slow majesty of the cosmos. The stars surrounded him like silver studs in the celestial vault. With him was his immortal mate, Vera York.

Their earth-born love had transformed itself into a spiritual bond that made them almost one. They did not need food or air; their bodies were in a state of suspended animation. They lived only in the mind, exchanging thoughts by telepathy. Their ship drew illimitable power from the vast storehouse of energy with which space was crammed—the cosmic rays. Subtle warpings of the gravitational lines of giant, distant suns gave the ship lightning motion. Unbound by the blind rules of Earthly science, they had often, and at will, exceeded the speed of light. On and on they had gone, nomads of the cosmos.

At times they had slowed and visited other planetary systems, had held concourse with alien races. Life exhibited itself to them in a hundred strange, incredible ways. Minds existed in the Universe whose thought processes were unfathomably queer. Never had they felt any kinship with other intelligences. And never, in all their Brobdingnagian journeying, had they found any planet system quite like the Sun's, nor any world quite like Earth.

Suddenly they knew what it was. Immortal they might be, abhuman and superhuman, children of space itself, but they could not deny what it was—nostalgia! They had lived in space five times as long as on their birthworld, yet on the way back they knew they were heading—home! A warm pulse-beat rose in their brains as they neared the little yellow-white star buried near the hub of the gigantic pin-wheel of the Milky Way Galaxy.

When the Sun had begun to enlarge among the stars, Anton York willed himself out of his hypnotic state of bodily suspension. Mind-controlled relays turned on the various mechanisms that supplied heat, air, and artificial gravity. His lungs took in a deep, shuddering breath, the first in several years. His heart suddenly began rumbling in his chest. Congealed blood, bearing the Elixir-enzyme, began to circulate to body cells whose radiogens drew life-energy from the cosmic rays.

His wife, Vera, joined him a moment later. They embraced, and drank the thrill of corporeal existence. Their ship was once again a living room, after being a cold, preserved coffin for the years of their swift journey through remotest space.

York consulted his instruments and made rapid mental calculations.

"We've been gone from the Solar System just one thousand and one years, Earth scale," he announced. "When we left here we were thirty-five years old, physically. And that's exactly how old we are on our return—physically. Of course mentally, spiritually, we're much, much older. We've *lived* some, haven't we, Vera?"

"Gloriously, Tony!"

"Odd that we've come back here, to this drab little planet system. Remember the grand system of the triple suns—one white, one orange, one red—with its fifty-six gigantic planets? And yet, in a way, I'm glad to be back here."

"There's no place like home," quoted Vera gaily. She knew she was going to enjoy the revival of old memories and associations.

York wheeled the ship in a course high above the plane of the Solar System, as they approached, adopting a wide-swinging parabolic course. Soon dark and gloomy Pluto appeared among the stars, grew to high magnitude, then faded in the rear. Pinkish Neptune with its one great moon paraded past their ports, like a will-o'-wisp. Steel-grey Uranus, with its smoky atmosphere, exhibited four huge satellites, considerably off to one side.

York cut obliquely and swept over xanthic Saturn with its brilliant Rings and brood of moons. Vera studied the sight with their ship telescope, remarking that for sheer beauty the Saturnian system was unmatched in all space.

Cyclopean Jupiter hove to, an agate striped with brownish bands, the largest of planets with the largest number of satellites. They had seen monster planets beside which Jupiter would be a pea, but somehow, for sheer impressiveness, this great planet was second to none. Vera, gazing at it through the telescope, expressed her admiration. The four largest moons glinted brightly not far out from their primary. The smaller satellites were fainter, but distinguishable from the pinpoint stars by their small discs.

Suddenly Vera looked up.

"Tony," she asked puzzledly, "how many moons did Jupiter have?"

"Ten—and still should have."

"That's what I thought." Vera bent her eyes to the binocular sights again. "Strange," she declared after a moment, "only nine moons are there now!"

"What? That's nonsense!"

"Look for yourself."

York looked, and counted. He saw the first small Jovian moon, close to the planet like a tiny silver flea preparing to land. Further out, in order, were the four largest moons, Io, Europa, Ganymede and Callisto. Seven times as far was another small moon. Twice as far out as this were two still smaller satellites. And a little further out, the last. Their total was nine. Obviously, one was missing. But which one was it?

Not trusting to memory—memory that would have had to reach back a thousand years—York rummaged through his chart closet and retrieved an old astronomical book. He turned to a diagrammatic picture of the Jovian system and compared the printed orbits to imaginary ones in the telescopic view. The missing moon was number six, a small one of perhaps a hundred miles diameter, whose orbit had been more than seven million miles from Jupiter's surface.

"Some mystery here," York muttered, straightening up. "A moon just can't go disappearing like that. We've been away a thousand years, yes, but that moon revolved in its orbital groove for millions of years before that!"

What did the missing moon of Jupiter signify? A clue revealed itself several hours later, as the Jovian planet drew steadily nearer. York had turned on his powerful radio receiver and listened to the amazingly clipped speech that vibrated through the ether. Evidently the English language, though universally used, had suffered considerable alteration. Listening carefully, York realized it had been brightened and made more flowing. Undoubtedly their speech would sound archaic to these people of the 31st Century.

Suddenly a powerful, booming voice had blanketed other stations and vibrated throbbingly from the loudspeaker. Its production must have cost a fortune in power. It was a cold, hard, emotionless voice, with arrogant inflections.

"People of the Solar System!" it said. "And particularly, Councilors of Jove! You are aware, undoubtedly, that the number six satellite of Jupiter has vanished from its age-long orbit about its primary. Where is it, you ask. It is at present a good many millions of miles from its former position and is still moving away. This phenomenon is unprecedented. You wonder what inconceivable, but natural, force has done this."

The speaker paused and then went on dramatically: "It is not a natural force! It is man-made! Your lost Moon has been dragged away from its pri-mary—literally—by means of a force-beam and a supremely powerful en-gine. I, the Immortal, built this super-engine and moved a world! My price for the return of this satellite will be complete rule of the Solar System!"

The voice became ominous: "I have demonstrated that I have in my hands illimitable power. If I can move worlds, I can destroy worlds! My demands are not unreasonable, for I have the wisdom of ages, far more than any other living man. I have lived more than a thousand years. I am immor-tal, and all-powerful. You will have twenty-four hours in which to discuss this matter, and arrange to call a council at which I will be made emperor. The Immortal waits."

"Did you hear that—*the Immortal!*" gasped Vera. "Is it possible that he is one of Vinson's group? Or has the Elixir been rediscovered?"

"It's one or the other," mused York. "The removal of a satellite from its orbit is no bluff. It's quite a feat, even though it is a comparatively small body. Whoever that person is, he's dangerous."

He stroked his brow thoughtfully.

"Vera, I had planned to go directly to Earth, to spend a few quiet years there. Incognito, of course. And then to stock up on supplies. But instead I think we'll hover around Jupiter and see the outcome of these amazing cir-cumstances." His eyes narrowed. "Unless the human race has changed a lot since our time, there's going to be resistance to the Immortal's challenge for supremacy. And after that—trouble!" Promptly when the twenty-four hours were up—Earth-scale being standard in the System—the Immortal's boom-ing radio voice came again from the depths of space, demanding to know if his ultimatum had been accepted. York listened carefully for the reply, which came after a certain time lapse because of the distances involved.

"The council of Jove, representing the Supreme Council of Earth and the Solar System, declines to accept your terms.

"You, the Immortal, are hereby declared an outlaw and a traitor. As such, you will be hunted and destroyed by our Space Patrol. If you will restore the sixth satellite of Jupiter to its rightful position, and give your person into custody, the ultimate sentence will be lightened."

For answer, a grating laugh came from the Immortal.

"I have been declared an outlaw by several other provisional governments in the past thousand years, but I have never been apprehended." The voice suddenly spat fire: "You will take the consequences of your answer. The missing satellite is thirty millions of miles from Jupiter. It will be returned to you—as a projectile! At the speed of a thousand miles a second, it will crash into Ganymede and destroy it! That is my answer!"

York snapped off the radio and turned to Vera with horrified eyes.

"He's a madman!" exclaimed Vera. "Tony, can't we do something about this? After all, these are our people; this is the world of our birth. We can't stand by and see an inhabited world destroyed!"

York sprang to his feet.

"We will do something!"

Chapter 3

York bent over an instrument whose readings indicated that the Immortal's message had come from the direction of the Sun. Then he stepped to the telescope and scoured the region thirty million miles Sunward from Jupiter. He discovered it among the numberless stars, in the belt of Orion near giant blue Betelgeuse—a small half-disc. It was the lost moon.

York then seated himself at the pilot board and touched studs that guided huge gravitational stresses through his engine. Following a course he had already calculated in his mind, he drove his ship in smooth acceleration toward the tiny, lost moon. Like a ball from some cosmic musket, the ship hurtled Sunward.

Inside, nothing was felt of the tremendous, crushing acceleration York had applied. He had long before solved the secret of inertia-suspension. They could have leaped from a cruise to the speed of light in one second without the slightest discomfort.

An hour later their destination loomed large in their front port. It had moved position—toward Jupiter. The Immortal had already begun its furious thrust, aimed it like a titanic cannonball for Ganymede. He had said he was doing it by means of a force-beam—a closed beam of artificial force which could be made more rigid and gripping than a solid bar of steel. York had used small force-beams himself, at times, to anchor his ship above strange worlds whose surfaces were not attractive for landing.

But this Immortal's force-beam was one designed to move a world. Only one force was capable of moving a world—another world's gravity field. He was either pulling it, or pushing it, by means of some great gravity field. If pulling, he was using Jupiter's gravity field. If pushing, he was drawing power from the distant Sun's field. Figuring rapidly, York decided he was probably doing the former, since Jupiter was so much nearer and more effective.

He slowed his ship's mad pace and took up an orbital path around its Jupiter side. If the Immortal was on this side at all, he must be at one certain spot—the spot bisected by an imaginary line drawn from the center of the moon to the position in Jupiter's orbit where Jupiter would be in twelve hours, and where Ganymede would be an hour later.

His quarry's distance from the moon's surface was one factor York could not foretell. It depended purely on the design of the force-beam projector he used. Thus, although York had the search narrowed down geographically, he had to hunt hit-or-miss in the third dimension spaceward from the lost moon's surface.

York wasted four precious hours searching for the invisible, silent, undetectable space-tractor with which the Immortal was catapulting the lost moon homeward. He spent only an hour on the Sunward side, where the sunlight would have quickly revealed any lurking ship. All this while the derelict moon's speed increased and it had already negotiated half the distance to Jupiter. In another five hours—

"The proverbial needle in the hay-stack," York muttered to his wife. His face was strained. Suddenly he snapped his fingers. "We'll have to take a chance," he said grimly.

The chance of being crushed by the terrific force-beam itself, designed to handle millions of tons of mass with toy-like ease. York simply shuttled his ship back and forth over the general area under which the force-beam must be anchored. He rode ten miles over the surface, to give himself leeway. His weaving course would eventually run him into the path of the force-beam.

It came finally—a furious wrench that made the entire ship groan and creak. It spun violently and dashed groundward at lightning speed, caught in the world-moving force of the beam. Securely strapped in their seats, York and Vera felt as though they were being torn apart. Their inertia-suspension was not equipped to neutralize rotary motion. Vera fainted. York, with an effort of will, clawed at the controls and stopped their twisting plunge a hundred feet above the brittle, rocky surface of the lost moon.

Vera came to almost immediately, smiling gamely. York was exultant.

"Now we have him located!" he cried.

He adopted a course perpendicular to the spot they had nearly crashed upon, crawled up into the starry vault. Twenty-five miles above the surface the Immortal's ship appeared among the stars. It was a gigantic thing with two enormous, bulging tubes at its back. From one of these was projected the force-beam. It returned to the other tube after passing into the center of the planet below and firmly gripping it.

The motion of this moon-and-ship system was accomplished by creating an unbalanced strain of its appreciable gravitational field in relation to mighty Jupiter. As a stretched rubber-band tends to snap together, so the distended force-field strained to close the gap between.

With fights out in his cabin, York pulled close to the dark ship. Into his meteor-screen he phased in another screen, one that was supersensitive to electromagnetic waves of high power. It would allow transmission of the low-power radio waves, but any radiation of high power would cause it to snap on instantaneously an impenetrable blanket screen. This protective wizardry had many times saved York out in space among hostile races.

Idling next to the huge space-tug, York radioed across.

"Anton York calling the Immortal. I am just outside your side ports, a hundred feet away. Reduce speed immediately and reverse your force-beam."

Evidently the Immortal had had his radio set open and heard, for his laugh sounded.

"The Space Patrol, eh?" his voice hissed. "Take that—"

There was a sharp click in York's cabin, which cut off the radio voice abruptly. An eye-searing shower of sparkles blossomed where the Immortal's lethal beam of exploding neutrons had impinged on the protective screen. Again the sparkles cast a lurid glare over the two ships, and revealed an amazed face at one of the larger ship's ports. A third time the high-powered beam expended itself against the impenetrable screen of York's ship.

York broadcast as the trigger-touch relay screen released the stronger one.

"You can't destroy me. My screen is beam-proof. But I can destroy you, Immortal!"

A gasp came from the radio.

"What did you say your name was?" asked the Immortal, as though suddenly realizing he had heard the strange name before.

"Anton York."

"Anton York! Not the—"

"Yes, the same Anton York who left the Solar System a thousand years ago. The York who annihilated the armada of the Immortals, of which you are apparently a survivor. Remember the weapon I had—the one which turned the Immortals' ships to black dust? I still have that weapon!"

"W-what do you want?" came the Immortal's cowed voice.

"I told you before. Reverse your force-beam and slow down the moon you are dragging. Then you will take up the course I plot, which will return this moon to its former orbit as the sixth satellite of Jupiter. One slightest infraction of my orders and I will turn you and your ship to—black dust!"

* * * *

Ten hours later the lost moon of Jupiter was restored to its age-old berth in the Jovian system, none the worse for its strange journey. It had not been inhabited nor even exploited for minerals. When York was satisfied that it had been given the right orbital speed to continue revolving properly, he allowed the Immortal to disengage the force-beam.

"You are coming with me now," stated York. "You have been branded an outlaw and must be turned over to the courts for sentence. Be thankful your crime hasn't been the destruction of Ganymede, as you originally intended."

But Mason Chard, recovering from his first awe and fear at the appearance of the legendary York, had been thinking—and scheming. When he released his force-beam from the planetoid, he coincidently shortened its focus. Then he made his ship wobble as though he were clumsy at the controls. At the proper moment, when York's ship was at his back, he jerked the levers and clamped his force-beam to it. Yelling in triumph, Mason Chard twisted his ship in circles, whirling York's like a stone at the end of a string. He released it suddenly.

It receded into the starry background and dwindled to nothingness. Chard hastily rammed full power into his engines, to make good his escape. He took a course directly away from York's ship, eager to put as much distance between as possible. That, he realized soon after, was a mistake.

When York was able to stop the flight of his ship and return to the spot where his prisoner had been, the other ship was long out of sight. It angered him that he had been tricked so easily. On the long chance that the other's psychology had been to dash the other way, York immediately gunned his ship in the same line, with furious acceleration.

He turned his meteor-screen to full power, for its protection, and scanned the dark regions ahead. A mounting velocity that had never been matched in the Solar System before overhauled the fleeing ship in a few minutes. York smiled grimly as a black shape ahead occulted stars like an expanding balloon.

Realizing his stupidity at the last moment, Chard veered his ponderous ship into a parabola. But York's ship clung near him as though attached by a chain. When Chard, in desperation, tried again to focus the powerful force-beam on his pursuer, a hazy beam of violet stabbed from York's ship, sheering off the force-beam projector neatly. The fused beam of ultra-sound and gamma-radiation turned the metal it touched into black dust, as it had turned to black dust fifty Immortal ships more than a thousand years before.

Chard gaped at the instruments which told of destruction in the rear part of his ship and turned white. Hastily he snapped on his transmitter.

"Don't destroy me!" he pleaded. "I surrender, York!"

"Very well," said York grimly. "Let's report to the Jovian Council. Head for Ganymede. I'll follow."

Chard had no alternative. Bitterness charged his heart as he swung toward Jupiter, completely subdued. The blow to his puffed ego made tears of helpless anger well to his eyes.

If the Jovian Councilors on Ganymede had been amazed at the disappearance of their moon, they were still more astounded at its sudden reappearance. The fears of the panic-stricken inhabitants of Ganymede were quieted. Had this all been a huge practical joke by that queer, half-mythical person who had flitted in and out of history during the past thousand years? Or did it have a deeper significance. Many there were who did not believe in the existence of Mason Chard, explaining it as a recurrent fable dating from the time of the Immortals a thousand years before.

An attendant approached the Chief Councilor and whispered in his ear. The latter looked at the attendant as though he thought him insane, but at his earnest look nodded and sent him away. Then the Chief Councilor turned to his colleagues and raised a hand. His face was bewildered.

"Gentlemen," he said in a high-pitched voice, "we are to be honored with the presence of the Immortal, the man who recently threatened this world with destruction! And his captor is a certain—Anton York!"

A dead silence came over the room. Every face looked incredulous. Anton York, the greatest figure in past history—the immortal who had given mankind the secret of controlled gravitation. And then, more a god than a man, had plunged into outer space, no longer concerned with the petty affairs of men. *He* was here?

The silence became more impressive, if that were possible, as York strode into the room, followed by his dejected looking prisoner. York stood before them, a man of thirty-five years of age, tall, strong, virile. Physically he was no different from any other man in the prime of life, but he carried an aura of superintellect that was immediately noticeable. The Councilors felt themselves shrinking mentally.

"You say you are Anton York," stammered the Chief Councilor, trying to be officious. "But what proof have you—" He broke off, staring fascinatedly into York's wisdom-filled eyes. "You *are* Anton York!" he whispered, in stark realization that he could be no other with eyes like that.

York told his story, in what to them was queerly archaic English. At the end he gestured to Chard. "He is your prisoner," York concluded. "His sentence will be in your hands."

Mason Chard said nothing. He seemed utterly deflated in spirit. But his eyes glared at York with a world of hate toward this man from the past who had come back like a ghost to spoil his plans. York stared back dispassionately. They stood thus, eye to eye, for a long minute. Two immortals from a long-ago era, meeting in a far future to find themselves opposed in aim and purpose. All the things of their time were dead and forgotten, except as history, but here they stood, a millennium later, to find themselves natural enemies.

The Chief Councilor tried to look sternly at the Immortal, but was awed by him, too. This man had eluded the forces of law and order in the Solar System for one thousand years. At last guards were called in, to conduct him to a prison for later trial.

"And now, sir," said the Chief Councilor, turning to York, "on behalf of the Supreme Council of Earth, the here-present Council of Jove, and the united peoples of the Solarian Empire, may I extend our deepest gratitude for—"

York waited patiently while the Chief Councilor, rising to the occasion, went on in this vein for several minutes. When he stopped for breath, York acknowledged the speech with a few polite words and then asked a question.

"Has the secret of immortality been rediscovered?"

"No," replied the Councilor. "Mason Chard, the only Immortal alive today, was from the original group of the 20th Century."

Within himself, York sighed in relief. His father had been fortunate to stumble on one of the greatest secrets of the Universe, the secret of immortality. Pure, blind luck it had been, probably, against all the laws of chance. Better that the secret never again be discovered. It had caused sufficient trouble at one time. It had more possibilities of harm than good, as exemplified by Dr. Vinson's disastrous scheme, and now this Mason Chard's subversive career.

York stayed with the Jovian Council, an honored guest, to ask many more questions. He had heard the histories and doings of many queer peoples in interstellar space, but this one had the appeal of familiarity. He thrilled to the epic thousand years of mankind's advent in the Solar System.

Then, to see this great glory of man's dominance in the nine-world empire, he and Vera embarked on a tour of the planets. But they did not leave Jupiter until they had witnessed the trial of Mason Chard. The criminal seemed to have suffered a change of heart after his encounter with York. He promised that in exchange for his life, forfeit under the law, he would work as a scientist for the betterment of mankind. By a narrow margin, his request was granted. A plan was drawn up for a laboratory to be built on the sixth satellite of Jupiter, the very one he had tried to destroy, in which he would labor, under heavy guard.

"They had better make the guard strong enough," was York's private comment to his wife in their ship. "Mason Chard is not the one to be trusted. The memory of a thousand years of absolute freedom is going to irk him considerably as his prison years go by." He shrugged. "But that is their problem. You and I, Vera, will make a tour of the Solar System; see just what the posterity of our time has done. It will be something like viewing the handiwork of our children."

Their little globular ship was seen on every one of the worlds in the next year. The two immortals, everywhere looked upon with awe and wonder, were a little amazed themselves at the wideness of man's activity. Earth's sons were in evidence everywhere, in communities ranging from great spanned cities to little isolated outposts a million miles from nowhere, literally. No environment had proved too trying. No dangers too great. No difficulties too hazardous. No other race of beings equal or superior.

With little more than his bare nerve, man had gained a toehold on a variety of misfit worlds. It was the beginning of a truly colossal undertaking—the complete annexation of all the Solar System. On remote, frozen Pluto, a band of hardy scientists reconnoitered, for possible colonization, the wastes of that planet.

On the way back from Pluto to Earth, York became very thoughtful. "Vera," he said suddenly, "how do you suppose the colonists on Venus would like to have a moon in their skies?"

"What a crazy question!" said Vera, laughing. "Are you serious?"

"I was never more serious in my life," York objected. He went on musingly: "If Mason Chard did nothing else, he gave me a great idea. He moved a moon—a world! Man, in progressing, must either adapt to his environment, or change the environment to suit himself. Vera, Vera!" he cried. "Don't you see? Why not remake the Solar System to suit mankind?"

"But can they do it?" asked Vera, not quite grasping his meaning.

"They!" exclaimed York. "No—we! We can do it!"

Six months later York had completed his plans, stupendous plans which he presented to the Supreme Council on Earth in a simplified form. "All I will need," he told them, "is the one ship built under my instructions, and full cooperation in certain state matters that will arise later."

The Supreme Council, the rulers of all the empire, were stunned by the magnitude of the thing. They deliberated for two months. York was asked a million and one questions by experts and technicians who were called upon to give their opinion. York was patient until they asked him if there would be danger.

"Danger?" he snorted, eyes ablaze suddenly. "No more than in any other human endeavor. No more than the pioneers who first settle a wilderness. Or to the man who first landed on Pluto with a clumsy ship. Or to the dawnman who ventured into the next jungle. All progress is hard won. It is the human heritage. It is not a question of danger—it is a question of courage!"

The grant was given. The parts for the great ship were manufactured at various centers of industry on Earth and shipped to the assembly ground York had been granted, near Sol City, the capital of the Solarian Empire. Under his watchful eye, it grew as a zeppelin-shaped craft a mile in length. Its interior was a maze of machinery patterned after York's superscience. Only he understood their full possibilities.

Five years later it was launched, manned by a thousand picked space-men and technicians. It rose into the sky like a mammoth cigar and lumbered off into space. As it left Earth, its great bulk delayed the next eclipse of the moon a hundredth of a second—the only man-made thing ever to do this!

Chapter 4

York, alone with Vera in his private cabin which was perched like a conning tower above the nose, took pride in giving the orders that were to make a vision in his mind become reality. The Gargantuan ship eased past the orbit of Mars and approached the asteroids. Soon it passed asteroids which were far smaller and lighter than itself. Finally, the *Cometoid*, as it was named, hove to before Ceres, the largest of the asteroids, some 480 miles in diameter. A small colony of miners had already been safely taken away by another ship, leaving it deserted of human life.

The thoughtful-eyed man at the nose of the ship barked commands. A microphone carried his voice to all parts of the ship. A thousand men jumped to their duties. The ship's stern lined itself with Ceres. An invisible bond sprang from ship to asteroid. The ship moved, towing the miniature world with it. The space-tug pointed for Venus and gathered speed.

Ceres, carted those 250,000,000 miles, was installed in an orbit close enough to Venus to allow its brilliant reflection to shine through the misty atmosphere. Thus Venus was given a moon to the delight of its warmth-loving inhabitants. The success of the macro-cosmic engineering feat gave York the same sublime feeling he had had a thousand years before, when he had first realized he was immortal. It was the beginning of a revamping of the Solar System. The astro-engineers of the *Cometoid* piloted their ship back to the asteroid belt and picked Pallas away. This 300-mile planetoid was given to Mars as a moon, to supplement its two tiny, inconspicuous ones.

Then something else was tried. York, long a lover of the majestic beauties of deep space, knew the value of beauty in man's life. The brilliant spectacle of Hailey's Comet—faithfully returning every seventy-six years for untold centuries—inspired the next Herculean task. If a comet was such an entrancing panorama when it passed close to Earth or any other planet, why not make this spectacle grander and oftener?

No sooner said than done—with York and his science. Calculations of almost infinite intricacy gave the elements of an orbit that would bring the next comet closely, but neatly, by Earth, Venus and Mars. It was not much of a trick, comparatively speaking, to fasten the end of a force-beam to the comet's nucleus and drag it into its new track around the Sun.

The first one, unfortunately, was lost in the Sun, but the next eight were more carefully warped into their new grooves of motion. After that, all the peoples of the inner planets—which held the bulk of the Empire's population—were to be treated to brilliant cometary displays at least once a year.

The Empire applauded this miraculous bit of Universe-building and waited avidly for the next. York next directed his wonder-ship out toward Jupiter. This great planet's nearest satellite, a small one, was evacuated by its small population and dragged to within two diameters of the primary. There was some doubt over the issue but finally the giant planet's gravitational stress obeyed the immutable laws of space and ripped the body to shreds, slowly scattering them in ring formation above its equator. Thus Jupiter had the same halo of glory Saturn had enjoyed for countless ages.

York's next undertaking was to give Mercury a period of rotation. Burying the end of a force-beam deep within Mercury, as an unshakable anchorage, York diverted the tremendous gravitational stress of the nearby Sun to one side of the planet. York's ship acted only as the medium of transfer of energy, not as the actual mover. Like the copper wire leading electricity to the motor, York's engines tapped the cosmic tanks and poured their world-moving powers into the field of operation.

Slowly but certainly the surface of Mercury began to rotate under the Sun's rays. Two years of this finally gave the Sun's first planet a day and night of forty hours each. With the more equal distribution of sun-heat and space-cold on its two formerly unmoving hemispheres, the entire planet was made habitable, instead of just the narrow twilight zone. It went into the annals of the Empire's history as a unique experiment in world-moving.

Then York revealed for the first time that he had atomic power available on his ship—the form of energy that had stubbornly defied man's efforts to pry it loose from its matrix of matter. He must be truly a god, he who had that!

York embarked on the second part of his superproject of interplanetary landscaping. Much of Mercury's surface was given a baptism of supernal fire. Atomic-powered pulverizer-beams transformed its hitherto drab, uninspiring harshness of rock areas into a garden bed of nutritious soil. Hardy plant forms were later to be sown abundantly, to soften the bleakness of the vast calcite plains.

Moving to Venus, York clarified its smoky atmosphere by chemically stripping from it millions of tons of water vapor, carbon dioxide, and the granite dust that arose from its violent wind storms. This took five years, positioned high in the atmosphere, spraying waste products out into space at a speed which insured their departure forever.

Mars was next carefully surveyed, for the purpose of filling its long empty sea bottoms. By repair and extension of its monumental canal system, some polar water had been forced equator-ward by the colonists. But only a faint trickle had got into the sea bottom. Warning everyone away from the polar regions, York swung a tremendous heat ray down on the age-old ice.

With a master's touch, he produced a head of water that snaked over the flat lands and eventually poured into those ancient hollows that may once have floated a lost civilization's ships, millions of years before. The process, repeated at the other pole, filled the sea bottoms to great depths and duplicated on a miniature scale the oceans of Earth.

All these feats on a planetary scale were measured in years. At times the *Cometoid* had to be grounded for repairs, refueling, restocking with supplies and men. For men died in this service, with the passing years, and had to be replaced with younger, fresher forces. But York and Vera, eternally young, knew nothing of the passage of time except as a mathematics of the mortal mind. To them, the rebuilding of the Solar System filled the space of a day in their long, long lives.

York turned the *Cometoid's* blunt prow toward the major planets again. Jupiter's poisonous atmosphere was swept clean of its venomous gases by a series of enormous suction machines, like vacuum cleaners, which converted the obnoxious molecules into solid precipitates that fell to the ground. Because the Jovian planet was such a huge one and its atmosphere so extensive, this cleansing took ten years. But for future ages, people would be able to wander freely over its tremendous surface in their levitation shoes.

Io, Jupiter's moon, was scoured sweet from its deadly, tenacious fungi by a tongue of protonic flame.

Saturn's ammoniated atmosphere was suitably neutralized by a two-year belching forth of hydrogen-chloride gas from leviathan gas chambers. York's chemical stores were all produced by transmutation of nearby and often surrounding raw products.

The bitter coldness of Uranus' frosty surface was relieved by deep and wide shafts that brought up the planet's internal heat. York dug the shafts by means of a pillar of livid atomic energy that disintegrated matter at almost the solar rate.

Neptune offered the tricky problem of being completely covered with a hundred-foot layer of solidified and liquefied gases. This had not prevented daring souls from living in this inimical environment in completely self-sufficient arks that floated over these bitter seas. York did not pass the challenge. After all the residents had been warned away, he dropped innumerable bombs of atomic flame deep in the frigid fluid wastes.

For two years Neptune was a flame in the heavens to rival the Sun as the brilliant atom-fire burned its way through all the surface sea, dissipating most of it into space. The planet's true surface was revealed for the first time in incalculable ages, to become the dwelling grounds in the future of Earth's ever pressing hordes.

York carried his mighty tools lastly to remote Pluto, some four billion miles from the Sun. Perhaps in the future, man, who could carry his air and heat with him, might find reason to inhabit this dark and cold planet. Here he chiseled down and smoothed over a surface that had been violently tossed into jagged upheaval by the long-ago interaction of its molten mass and the sudden chill of space.

When this was done, York raised the *Cometoid* above Pluto and contemplated his work, here and in the rest of the Solar System. He felt a deep glow of pride. Then he swung his eyes out beyond Pluto, out toward the distant immensity of interstellar space. Into his eyes came a strange look, a yearning for the greater freedom of the macrovoid.

"Our work here is done," he said to Vera.

"Yes," said Vera. "Well done." She too was gazing out at the unplumbed infinity in which they had lost themselves for a thousand years—for a magnificent second of eternity.

"We will go out there soon," said York. "By the way," he continued, "how long have we been at this work—in the time scale of Earth?"

"Fifty years," answered Vera. They both laughed, then, at the meaningless words.

The giant, blunt ship left Pluto and with ponderous grace hurtled toward the dim, distant Sun. York landed it at Ganymede for repairs. It was here that he heard the news of Mason Chard's escape from imprisonment.

"I knew that would happen," he said to the Councilors, shaking his head. "You should have executed him. Now you will have him on your hands again, stirring up trouble for the next thousand years, as he has for the past thousand. Well, that is your problem. If I knew any way of finding him, I'd go out after him. But of course, he's far too clever to run across my path again."

Escape had seemed impossible, at first, to Mason Chard. He had been isolated in an underground laboratory on Jupiter's sixth moon, watched over day and night by armed guards. The exits above had been policed, and overhead a Space Patrol ship had kept close watch for possible rescue by confederates.

But Mason Chard had had no confederates. He had at times hired unscrupulous men in certain projects, but never had he entrusted them with his full plans or retained them. Immortal and conceited, he felt himself above human ties. He did not know the meaning of the term friend. As a lone wolf he had pursued his way and so it would be to the end.

For fifty years he had waited for his chance to escape. His scientific endeavor for his captors, on which promise he had won his life, amounted to little. His was not the keen scientific brain, but simply an average one. He was, in the last analysis, a common man with the gift of immortality. He had amused himself in the past thousand years in the way a coarse mind would—by playing god with the people whom he outlived century after century.

Chard's escape was typical of his ruthlessness. He had surreptitiously put together bit by bit a miniature of the same weapon he had developed for his space ship. It charged itself with the energy of the cosmic rays and was able to release it in short, concentrated blasts of exploding neutrons, before which nothing human could stand.

Chard killed his personal guards without compunction. Donning a space suit, he made his way to the exit and burned down the three men there. When the members of the landed Space Patrol ship came on the run to investigate, the superior range of his weapon gave Chard the victory. Their ship was his means of escape from the sixth satellite.

Chard allowed all the bitterness of his fifty years of incarceration to come out in one short, harsh laugh, as the prison satellite faded from his view. They would pay for the humiliation it had cost him, these mortals! When York had left the System and gone far out into space, then Chard would act.

The Immortal had not been out of contact with events in the Solar System for the years of his imprisonment. He was granted the use of a radio and televisor and had watched with avid interest York's remolding of the Solar System. Safe in his secret hideout in the deepest crater of Earth's moon—which had been unmolested for the fifty years of his absence—Chard now watched the ceremonies attendant to York's landing on Earth, his mission finished.

"Why has he done all this?" wondered Chard. "Is he planning to ingratiate himself with the people of the Empire, so that they will offer him a throne? Has he come back from remote space to wrest from me my dream of ten lifetimes?" Always theatrical in his thoughts, from a thousand-year inflation of ego, Chard's eyes blazed as he concluded: "Is there to be a battle of the gods for this kingdom of mortals? If so, let *him* beware! He has bested me once, by a trick, but I've not tested my full powers!"

Despite this boast, however, Chard felt a strong relief as the televized image of York, standing on a tall marble platform before a sea of faces at Sol City, said:

"People of the Solar System! As the city-planner levels and prepares his city-site, so have I prepared the Solar System for the future Empire of mankind, and his subject races. But when the city-planner is done with his work, he does not seek or accept the rule of the city he has made possible. That is for the city itself to do. The Supreme Council has offered to relinquish authority. You people have petitioned me for ruler. The crown has been offered me, but I must decline, even though it is the greatest crown in the history of man. We are going out into fathomless space again, my wife and I. It is our destiny!"

Chard's eyes gleamed in satisfaction. That would make things simpler for him.

After the crowd's low moan of disappointment had subsided, York spoke again, waving an arm toward the huge, shining bulk of the *Cometoid* nearby in its landing cradle.

"I leave you this legacy," he said. "It is an instrument which may yet prove of further use to you. I have left full and complete instructions for its operation and functions in the control chamber. I only ask that you practice care when you make use of the *Cometoid*. It can be a mighty engine of world-destruction, if used wrongly, or carelessly. Its powers are like the sinews of Jovian-sized Titans. Rightly applied on the other hand, it can be of inestimable utility, in ways comparable to the things I have done with it in the past fifty years."

Chard's eyes had narrowed, looking at the *Cometoid*. The thoughts it conjured up were so intense that he failed to hear York's short and final farewell speech. He was suddenly aware of the televisor scene broadening to show a tiny, globular ship leaping into the sky. A million awed faces watched it dwindle to a pinpoint glistening in the sunlight, and then vanish completely.

As they arrowed away from Earth, the immortal couple were silent with their thoughts.

"You have done a great work, Tony," said Vera. She kissed him impulsively. "They will not forget it for all the ages to come." A slight frown came to her face. "But, Tony, do you think it wise to leave the *Cometoid* in their hands? It is such a powerful thing. And they are like children at times."

"Yes, it is wise," said York softly. "It is the only way." Pluto rolled by their ports after a time. Behind lay the nine-world empire of man. Ahead lay the vast void.

Chapter 5

Mason Chard bided his time patiently. He would wait a full year for York to plunge far, far into the void. So far that no chance message could leak out to him and bring him back. For the success of his present plans, it was essential that the one being who could possibly disrupt them was totally out of the picture. Mason Chard waited a long year, a year that seemed longer to him than the previous hundred had been.

In that time, he perfected his plans with a finesse that assured triumph barring a remote unlucky chance. Delving into the vast worldly riches he had accumulated throughout his extended lifetime, he circulated among the scattered space-ports. Keeping his identity utterly secret, he hired a man here and there. He picked them carefully—bitter, disappointed souls whose careers had not been untainted, yet whose abilities as spacemen at one time had been, or still were, respected. Knowing human nature as he did, from a thousand years of observation, he could readily choose men whose cupidity was great and conscience small. Swearing each to utter secrecy, he had them congregate quietly and singly, as he met them, at his Lunar lair.

Through the centuries, he had at other times banded together similar groups, at the other hidden quarters throughout the Solar System. Yet never before had he picked so carefully, nor so many, nor for so stupendous a reason.

At last he had over two thousand men under his banner. Finally, with the entire band before him in his Lunar headquarters, Chard revealed his identity. The hardened, laconic men-of-fortune were not too surprised.

But when he laid bare his reason for having them together, they were completely dumfounded. It was something that made them gasp. Chard spoke at some length. Surprise gave way to interest. Interest to avarice when he began to list the rewards that would follow. When Chard saw that he had won the majority over, he requested those who wished to withdraw to step away from the main crowd.

Some twenty men gathered together at one side of the huge underground chamber, expecting safe departure in return for a promise of secrecy. Chard calmly pulled out the hand weapon in his belt. A livid beam of exploding neutrons sprang toward the unlucky men, sprayed back and forth. In a minute a score of blackened bodies sprawled grotesquely. When the last screams of agony had died away, Chard sheathed his gun and turned to the silent group who had watched this wanton carnage.

"That," he said ominously, "is to prove I mean business."

* * * *

The large armed force guarding the giant drome that had been built around the *Cometoid* was not prepared for the sudden, vicious onslaught that came out of the night sky. A half hundred silent ships dropped in their midst and sprayed fiery death. While this was going on, half the ships landed next to the drome and deposited small figures which scurried into the huge structure, blasting their way through metal walls with powerful heat-bolts.

Mason Chard himself was in the lead, closely followed by a dozen men who had been part of the crew of the *Cometoid* years before. With their knowledge, they showed the way to enter the ship and swarm up its miles of corridors, by rail-car. Each of the dozen who knew the intricacies of the ship led a separate party in a separate direction.

An elevator took Chard and one other to the master control room. Quickly the other explained. Chard, veteran of space travel for a thousand years, soon had a working conception of the incredible craft's controls. York's amazing genius had reduced them to comparatively few. Then the ship's local communication system was switched on. In a short time, various sections of the ship began reporting that the men had grasped their duties and were ready to execute them.

Chard snapped on the exterior vision screen and the all-seeing electric eye beyond the drome. The guard had been utterly routed. Then he saw a unit of Earth's air police swoop down from the sky, answering an alarm. He watched as the half hundred well-armed ships staved off the more numerous attackers. The battle went on for long minutes. When reinforcements for the police arrived, the end was inevitable. But so Chard had expected. It had all been timed to the last minute.

When his ships outside had been cut down to half under the blasting guns of the police, Chard received the final report from the last, remote corner of the huge ship. He barked orders. A steady, low throb rumbled in the bowels of the great vessel, and its walls began to vibrate from the birth of great energies.

When the last ten of his outside ships broke under the police onslaught, Chard grasped a lever with a sweaty, but confident hand; pulled it over. The mighty ship leaped from the ground, grinding the drome to shreds. Chard left his remaining ships to the mercy of the air police. He grinned sardonically to think they had believed he would bother to save any left after the battle.

The *Cometoid*, a juggernaut of space, rose from Earth, manned by a thousand unprincipled scoundrels, captained by a ruthless, immortal demon. He might have been a demon from the way his evil eyes gleamed redly in triumph as he directed the captured ship toward the barren reaches beyond

Jupiter. Here, where passing ships were rare, the *Cometoid* hovered for a month, while its new masters familiarized themselves with it.

Chard had not slipped up on anything. He had known from spies that the ship was well-stocked and fueled. He had known that its creator's instructions on the full operation of the monster craft were stored in the helmroom.

Chard was astounded at the full scope of powers at his disposal. Sweeping atomic rays that could eat their way to the heart of a planet. Giant plants that could produce millions of cubic feet of violent gases, given suitable raw material. Powerful forcebeams that could grip mighty Jupiter himself and yank him from his age-old orbit. Energy-conversion machines which could store the dynamite of cosmic radiation and the slow, infinite power of gravitation.

Chard realized he had a truly godlike instrument in his hands, one that could make him master of ten universes, if he wished.

Chard's stentorian all-wave radio voice that burst into the broadcast channels of the Solar System carried the most startling message in all history:

"Mason Chard, the Immortal, speaks! I speak to all the Solar System, and to all of its so-called ruling element. My ship, the *Invincible*—formerly the *Cometoid*—hovers over the moon of Earth. You all know the illimitable powers of this ship, but I invite the eyes of Earth to watch the center of the moon, the mountain range known to astronomers as the *Apennines*. Watch it for the next hour!"

Millions of eyes on the night side of Earth watched and saw a small spark blaze in the center of the Lunar disc. It grew and widened until it was a fiery incandescent diamond, spewing out a shower of sparkles that spattered over the entire moon's face. Some terrific holocaust of supernal fire, comparable to the Sun's blazing furnace, was creating a deep, molten puddle on the moon!

Then the sparkles ceased and the voice continued: "This same beam of atom-fire can quite readily be focused on any city or spot on Earth, to reduce it to molten matter that will not cool for a week. Or on any planet in the Solar System! The *Invincible* has moved from the moon to Earth. It is now hovering over Sol City. Nothing can save it, if I decide to destroy this citadel of ruling power!"

To himself, Chard added: "Not even the once timely York, who is now trillions of miles beyond reach."

After a suitable pause, to allow the poison of fear to invade their minds, Chard continued:

"Does the Supreme Council of Earth, doomed at the flick of my finger if I so will it, have anything to say?"

Chard laughed triumphantly—

"No, but I have!"

Mason Chard choked in his laugh. Had his ears tricked him? Surely that had not been the voice of—

"Anton York speaking!" continued the quiet voice, inexorable as the stars. "Chard, you've just signed your death warrant. I knew you would try this sort of thing again. Unknown to you, the Council and I arranged, before I left Earth, to leave the *Cometoid* reasonably open to capture. You went for it, like a bee for its hive. You've been tricked, like any stupid fool. But it was necessary, for I could not leave the Solar System knowing you were at large, scheming. I've been hovering just beyond Pluto for the past year, waiting to trap you. It would be best if you would just quietly land the *Cometoid* and surrender yourself."

Chard's emotions racked his body. Dismayed to the roots of his being, his mind reeled on the verge of madness. A bitter acid seemed to eat its way to his brain and dissolve it. His gigantic ego wilted as overgrown weeds wilt under a hot sun.

His hand touched cold metal. It was a lever that could release, in one stellar blast, the awful power of tons of matter. Could York's little ship withstand it?

Chard sneaked a hand to his vision screen and twisted its knob rapidly. While the Solar System held its breath at this battle of wills between gods, he searched for York's ship. Presently he found it, a ridiculous pebble alongside the super-ship. Chard whispered orders into the local phone system, careful that his radio transmitter was off. Down below men fed giant powers into huge engines. Up above, a flaming-eyed man waited for the final moment. When it came, he jerked his levers with a desperate finality.

The frightful blast of energy that issued from one vent in the *Cometoid's* broad side engulfed York's ship and rammed it a mile backward. It should have blasted it to atom-debris. Chard turned a greenish white, for the little ship stopped, darted gracefully upward, and came back fully as fast as it had been flung away.

"Naturally, Chard, I was prepared for that," came York's unruffled voice. "Out in interstellar space, my screens have withstood forces far greater than those you've just released. Want to try again? But I warn you"—here for the first time the voice became a little ugly—"you will die sooner that way!"

Chard screamed a series of orders to his crew. The men, unknowing of anything going on outside their respective cells, obeyed with trained alacrity, thinking, if they thought at all, that perhaps the Space Patrol had attacked and needed a lesson.

All hell burst forth from the giant ship hovering over Earth. Some of its tremendous thunderbolts of destruction crashed down upon Earth's surface and gouged it horribly, killing many. But the ship at which the hellborne fury was directed continued to gleam in the starlight. It was no longer buffeted by the flaming energies that pounded at its protective screen. York had fastened a force-beam to the center of the ship. Now he began to swing in an arc, swifter and swifter, until he was revolving about the great ship, held tight by the force-beam.

York knew the ship, knew that its blind spot was in this path. None of the world-destroying forces could touch him here. He was able to open his defensive screen, which did not allow offensive rays to be given out, and retaliate at last. First he dragged the great ship along until it was no longer near Sol City. Then a faintly shimmering violet beam, representing the accumulation of a vast amount of cosmic rays, bit viciously into the hull. As York revolved, it neatly sliced the great ship in two, like a knife cutting a sausage.

Mason Chard, as he sensed what had occurred, became a madman. But the sudden sensation of falling jerked his mind, as great fears can at such times. He died the many deaths he had escaped in his many lifetimes as the ship fell, and knew at last that his immortality was ended…

The two halves of the mighty ship crashed with a sound that could be heard miles away in Sol City. It was the signal for rejoicing.

* * * *

As their ship sped away from the Solar System, fully stocked for the supertrek in galactic space, Vera sighed.

"It has been so diverting, so interesting, Tony! I hate to leave. It was a cross-section of the great drama of intelligence pitting itself against the blind, immutable forces of the Universe, to carve out for itself a lasting dominion. For the lone, fearful apeman, treading cautiously the threatening jungles of his origin to the bold daring man who placed foot on the last of nine far-flung worlds!"

York nodded. His eyes were misty as he scanned the infinite ahead.

"Yet it is all so petty, so small. There is a more supreme drama for us to witness out *there*. The sublime evolutions of suns and nebulae and the meta-galaxy itself. The riddle of eternity and infinity!"

Already their mental perspective had begun expanding to include the grandeur ahead. Earth and the Solar System receded to a sub-atomic mote in the incredible vastness of the void. A god and his mate were swallowed in its endless depths.

THE THREE ETERNALS

Chapter 1

On Mount Olympus, as all know who have read Greek mythology, live the gods. Jove, Mercury, Apollo, Bacchus, Neptune—their names are legion.

But there are not many gods, in a riotous confusion. There are but three. Immortal, and wise with the passing of time, these Three Eternals have looked over Earth and its folk at times, sometimes amused, sometimes angered, most often unconcerned.

They looked out upon the world of the Forty-first Century and were again unconcerned, though its inhabitants were doomed, unknown to themselves.

"Ah, these mortals and their absurd little civilization!" said one. "It is about time they and all they represent go into limbo—at our hand."

"It is dull waiting," yawned the second. "I wish—I actually wish—they knew of it, and challenged us. I would even wish a champion to appear for them. Anton York, for instance, who was greatest of them all."

"Anton York!" The third laughed. "He is far out in space. And if he were here, what could he do against us? Nothing!"

They smiled at one another, secure in that knowledge, and went back to their intricate game of four-dimensional chess, developed to help pass the slow crawl of time in their immortal lives…

Out in the vast, uncharted depths of interstellar space, a small globular ship plunged Earthward at a speed greater than light.

Within it, Anton York and his immortal mate grew hourly more eager. They were returning for a visit to the world of their birth, after a long absence. Like gods they had gone where they willed, viewing strange worlds, queer civilizations, taking deep pleasure in watching part of the majestic sweep of cosmic history.

Earth's individual history had faded in their minds, overlaid by countless other events, but now nostalgia tingled through their veins. Near-gods they might be, but even gods must have a place called "home."

"I can hardly wait to get back!" said Vera York, with all the enthusiasm of an American waiting to see the Statue of Liberty after a year in Europe. "Why have we stayed away so long, Tony?"

"How long has it been?" Anton York asked, vaguely.

"A thousand years!" Vera had checked the time-charts, amazed herself.

"That long?" York shook his head. "Time does fly, as an old proverb says. Yet, what is time to us? We will live, Vera, till half the Universe has run down into cosmic rays. Millions of years, at the least!"

It was bare truth. They were thirty-five years old—in appearance. In their bloodstreams flowed an elixir of self-renewing enzymes that constantly rebuilt radiogens, the tiny batteries of cell life. The boundless energy of all-pervading cosmic rays fed these radiogens, supplying the undying fires of youth to their bodies. Old age and disease could not touch them. The finger of Death could only mark them by violent means, if Fate so willed.

Vera shivered slightly.

"Millions of years!" she echoed. "Sometimes it isn't good to think of that." Her eyes, a little haunted, sparkled suddenly. "The first thing I'm going to do, when we arrive on Earth, is to take a swim in some cool mountain lake, surrounded by green trees. There will be birds singing, and soft warm breezes whispering through the leaves, and white clouds sailing on high—" She choked a little. "Oh, Tony, I'm just beginning to realize how much I miss those simple things!"

York nodded. In all their galactic roaming, there had been no world quite like Earth. No spot in the Universe quite so dear in their memories.

"We'll undoubtedly find a great civilization there on Earth," mused York, more practical-minded. "When we left, in the Thirty-first Century, mankind was already beginning to make the most of its nine-world empire. We'll find humanity in its happiest and mightiest phase since the first dawn-man built the first fire and found that Nature could be his ally. Mankind deserves it too, Vera, for all of its previous bickerings, maladjustments, and crimes against itself. Civilization went through its adolescence in the Twentieth Century, when we were born. Now it must be approaching maturity."

His eyes shone as he went on.

"And fully matured, mankind will one day inherit the stars! It will be destined to replace so many of the worn-out, decadent civilizations that fell by the wayside throughout the cosmos. But only when they are ready for it. As we have done in advance, the ships of Earthmen will seek far worlds and—"

"Tony, look! The bolide chart!"

Startled at his wife's sharp interruption, York turned to look.

The bolide chart was a luminous screen whose milky surface showed any and all material bodies within range. Nothing larger than a grain of sand could escape the super-sensitive instrument which recorded every tiniest ripple in the ubiquitous ether. With its train of mechanisms, the chart instantly recorded distance, speed, direction, size, shape, color and electrical charge of any passing object within the relatively close radius of a billion miles.

It was one of the precautions York had taken, with his scientific genius, to avoid accidents in treacherous space, so that their immortality was further safeguarded.

He watched the little black dot streaking across the lighted screen. At their tremendous speed, the passing object would be gone in seconds.

"No danger of collision with it," he said, integrating the data in his head. "It has a speed, relative to space, of a hundred thousand miles a second. Size, twice as large as our ship. Shape, quite uniform, elongated. Color, silvery. Direction, toward Alpha Centauri, from about Sol's position. Electrical charge—"

The dot slipped off the edge of the screen, beyond range.

"It's gone," said Vera. "First bit of matter we've passed in empty space, in days. Data sounded like a space ship, but of course it was only a lonely, wandering meteor of space. Maybe the next record will be that of the planet Pluto, within the Solar System. We're close now!"

York was strangely reflective.

"Yes, we're close—within a few trillions of miles. And therefore, it could be... Vera, I think it was a space ship! I barely caught its electrical charge record, and it seemed to be inordinately high—like that of a power-plant of some sort. Meteors don't have power-plants. If it was a space ship, does it mean that Earthmen have already achieved interstellar engines! And were they heading for Alpha Centauri, the nearest star to Sol? And what for?"

"We'll find out when we arrive at Earth," began Vera, but her immortal husband interrupted.

"We'll find out now!"

York snapped on his radio, twirling the dials of his transmitter. Underneath the cabin floor a great generator hummed to life. A million kilowatts of electrical power, drawn from the eternal shower of cosmic rays, surged through the radio's diamond-walled tubes.

The stentorian radio voice that burst from the antennae of his ship was borne by sufficient energy to be heard with the weakest of receptors within a light year. On Earth, that amount of power would have heated all metals within a mile ten degrees above their surroundings.

"Anton York calling the space ship heading for Alpha Centauri!"

After he had called over and over, without an answer, he frowned in perplexity and reached for the engine controls.

"I've got to find out about that ship," he muttered. "The fact that it doesn't answer is—ominous!"

With his inertia-suspension field on full power, York slowed his ship from its translight speed to zero in short hours, and shot back along the course of the mysterious ship. It was odd to find a ship out here in the depths between stars. He overhauled it in another few hours. They stared as it bulked huge against the backdrop of flaming stars.

It was unlighted, dark, but York's detectors showed that its power-plant was warping space and accelerating constantly. He tried his radio again, with no result. Then he sent a rocket signal over its bow, and when that failed, gave a baffled grunt.

"One of two things," he conjectured. "Its occupants are up to no good, or it's a derelict. We'll find out quick enough."

"Careful, Tony," warned his wife.

In a space suit, presently, York cautiously maneuvered himself toward the strange ship with his reaction pistols. Vera was covering him with their guns. But no sign of hostility came from the accelerating ship; no sign of life at all.

Finding a hatch with the usual outside emergency lever, York entered the ship. A hand flash lighted the way as he went down a darkened companionway into the main cabin. He gasped as his cone of light revealed the figures of two men lying unconscious against the back wall, as though they had been thrown there violently.

Unconscious? York had only to notice their utter stillness to realize they were dead!

Back in the other ship, Vera listened as York's voice came from his helmet radio, a half hour later.

"Listen, Vera! This is a first-class mystery. The crew of two are dead, from excess acceleration. The air is thin, barely breathable, very impure. Their food supplies are moldy. Water, evaporated. It's almost as though they had been holding out against terrific odds. Must have left Earth months and months ago, at their slow speed, less than light. Died trying to reach an impossible goal, light years away. Fools, they had no chance at all! Only a translight speed engine would do it. What drove them to this suicidal attempt at interstellar travel?"

His voice was half angered, half sorrowful.

"Daredevils there have always been," returned Vera. "Some, in Earth's history succeeded—Columbus, Byrd, Lindbergh—"

"Daredevils? Perhaps." York was preoccupied. "Strange, though that these men planned so poorly. And the haggard expressions on their faces, frozen in death, are those of men driven by some tremendous fanaticism. I wish I knew—"

Vera heard the soft indrawing of his breath, as he seemed to stoop, and then his voice again, excited.

"Vera, go into the lab and prepare the following injections, as I give instructions. Adrenalin—"

He went on, rapidly naming several rare compounds among his supplies, and giving the percentage of their solution.

"I'm coming across with one body," he said then. "Also have a bottle of oxygen ready. Hurry!"

"Tony, you mean—"

"Yes, reviving a dead man! One has been dead only an hour. He's still warm. Rigor mortis hasn't set in. But we'll have to hurry!"

Chapter 2

Twenty minutes later, Vera was handing York a hypodermic as they bent over the body of a man dead for more than an hour. Earthly science would have given the case up as hopeless. But York, with a knowledge of life forces garnished in several lifetimes of research, battled to bring back the spark of sentience. After a series of injections into the spine and heart, he waited. Powerful compounds were at work.

A fine dew of sweat beaded York's forehead. It was a slim chance, at the most.

Vera caught her breath suddenly.

A quiver ran over the corpse. A cheek muscle twitched. A low, hesitant thumping came into being in the quiet of the cabin. A beating heart! The ribs flexed suddenly, and the lungs gasped for breath.

York clapped a breathing cone over the man's nose and sent a stream of hissing oxygen into his lungs. The body quivered all over now, and suddenly the eyes flicked open, staring around blankly.

York took away the breathing cone, looking at the resurrected man a little proudly. He had run far into Death's territory and retrieved one of its victims!

"Can you speak?" York queried.

The vacant eyes paused on his for a moment, but only a broken gabble came from his lips.

Vera shuddered at the weird gibbering.

"Tony, you've brought back his body, but not his mind! It's horrible!"

York shuddered himself.

"But I've got to find out about the ship and journey," he insisted. "I'll try telepathy."

His brow furrowed as he concentrated on projecting a telepathic message. Within his left ear reposed a tiny instrument that could amplify brain waves enormously, his own or those of others. Sometimes he and Vera, for long periods of time, had communicated solely by telepathy, though it was mentally tiring.

York looked up at his wife after a moment, shaking his head.

"He doesn't respond coherently. His thought waves are completely disorganized. All I could pick out was some mysterious reference to the Three something. The Three Eternals, it sounded like."

Suddenly the gibbering of the resurrected man stopped. A look of sanity and awareness stole into his eyes.

"Who are you?" he asked quite clearly.

York had understood, though the man's accent was queer, the product of a thousand years' of language evolution since York had last been on Earth. He bent over the man eagerly.

"I'm Anton York," he returned, projecting the mental thought also, lest his archaic accent were not understood.

"Anton York!" The man's eyes widened, as a train of thought instantly followed that name.

The legendary Anton York! Two thousand years ago, in the Twentieth Century, he had been born, grown to the prime of life, and stayed there deathlessly, preserved by his father's life elixir. He had set out to solve the secret of gravitation, in three lifetimes of research. He had succeeded, but in the meantime the secret of his father's virus had been stolen.

York had fought and defeated fifty other Immortals before Earth was safe from their would-be overlordship.

Then he had gone out into space, he and his immortal wife, like gods.

They had returned. A thousand years before, in the Thirty-first Century, they had come back to find themselves again pitted against an Immortal who had survived York's vengeance against dictatorship. Before this renegade scientist had been sent to the death he deserved, York had performed the greatest man-made feats in all history.

Since the Thirty-first Century, Venus had a moon, also Mercury, and Mars had a third. York, world-mover, had done that. He had also formed rings for Jupiter, given Mercury a period of rotation, and relieved the harshness of most of the planets by suitable manipulations of heat, water, and gigantic natural forces. He had prepared the Solar System for mankind's dominion.

Then he had gone out into space again, drawn by its grandiose lure. A thousand years again he had not been heard from.

Now he was here once more, and the eyes of the revived man showed skeptical disbelief. Many there were, among Earth's people, who openly denied that any such man as Anton York had ever lived. It might well be, they said, an accumulative fable, involving the careers of dozens of mysterious scientists.

York caught all this from the man's startled mind. He smiled slowly.

"I'm Anton York, and I'm not a myth," he said quietly. "I've revived you from death, to find out about this mad journey you are making. Why were you going to Alpha Centauri, without adequate preparations?"

A look of horror suddenly flooded the man's eyes, as if just then recalling something.

"Civilization is doomed!" he said, his voice a dry croak. "There will be holocaust, destruction, all over Earth! The Three Eternals are doing it! We found out, tried to warn Earth. No one believed—we couldn't prove it. We hoped to reach Alpha Centauri, find planets to migrate to, save the race. Three Eternals—vicious demons—destroy civilization—doom—"

The voice became incoherent again, as though the ominous news he told had again driven his mind under.

York shook his shoulder.

"Tell me more!" he demanded. "Who are the Three Eternals? Where are they? Exactly what are they doing?"

"Three Eternals—gods of Mount Olympus—destroy all mankind—"

His voice trailed off into pure gibberish. A moment later his eyes glazed. His head dropped back and he fell into a second death, one from which even York's super-science could never rescue him.

Anton York and his wife arose, sadly.

"Gods of Mount Olympus destroying mankind!" Vera murmured. "It must have been some hallucination of his broken mind."

York turned a grave face.

"Maybe not, though! Civilization on Earth might really be in danger. The faster we get there and find out—"

In the following twenty-four hours that it took them to reach the Solar System, even at ten light speeds, the immortal pair were plagued by unrestful anticipation. They almost dreaded arriving now, perhaps to find some holocaust in progress on Earth, or already finished. The ship they had encountered had left Earth months before. What had happened in that time?

Sol, a comparatively mediocre yellow star in the hosts of heaven, became a sun. They swept past the dark outer planets. It thrilled them to see the splendor of Saturn's rings, unmatched in all the galaxy. Jupiter's rings, mark of York's last visit, thrilled them still more. Then past garnet Mars toward the green globe of Earth.

Familiar it all was to the two cosmic wanderers, but they hardly noticed. Earth occupied their thoughts—and the mysterious prophecy of doom on that planet. Yet nothing seemed amiss when they had dropped into the atmosphere layer.

A mile high, York halted his ship. Below them spread Sol City, the greatest metropolis of all time, with its fifty million inhabitants, the nerve center of the Solar System. It sparkled brightly in sunlight. Aircraft and space ships rose and descended from its many ports ceaselessly. It was bustling, vibrant, symbol of a busy, prosperous civilization.

There was nothing wrong here! York and Vera looked at each other in relief.

* * * *

There was an interruption in the sanctorum of the Solarian Council chamber, in the capitol of Sol City. A dozen gray-bearded men, executive ruling body of the Solar System, looked around in annoyance. Who had dared disturb them?

Through the opening door strode a tall man of erect bearing ignoring the protests of a clerk.

"We couldn't stop him, sirs!" stammered the clerk. "Not even the guards. He has some strange power!" The clerk bolted, as though unnerved.

The intruder walked boldly up to the council table.

"I wanted to see you gentlemen," he said calmly. "It's urgent. When the guards resisted me, I used certain telepathic powers that I have."

"Who are you?" demanded the president of the council, glaring.

"Anton York!"

The councilors smiled.

"Strange," mused the president, "how parents with the family name York have always baptized their sons Anton. It's a great name to carry through life."

"No, I'm the real Anton York. I came out of space a few hours ago."

The councilors looked at him narrowly. They started a little at his smoldering eyes. Insane! The asylums were filled with those who imagined they were the almost mythical Anton York as in an earlier age so many had identified themselves with Napoleon.

"Yes, of course," said the president gently, tapping his forehead for the benefit of his colleagues. "Now you just come with us—"

York could not blame them for not believing. But as they all converged on him, with the intent of hustling him out, he set his lips a little grimly.

"Sit down, all of you!" he commanded.

The men all stopped. Their faces were puzzled. Nothing tangible opposed them, yet they could not go on. Rulers of the Solar System, they turned back and sat down, impelled by a subtle force that could not be resisted.

"My mental commands must be obeyed, though I'm sorry I had to use them with you," York said firmly. "You must listen to me, whether you want to or not. I am the Anton York. I have the lore of the stars, and of two thousand years of time. I have some questions to ask."

Gasping, the councilors now realized it was the truth. The stranger's words were spoken with an archaic accent that alone tied him with a previous age. It was Anton York in person—stunning thought—returning to Earth after a thousand-year sojourn in the space that was his virtual home. The visitation was totally unexpected. They stared in awe at this immortal who had almost godlike powers at his command.

"I see you are finally convinced," resumed York. "Now tell me, does any danger threaten civilization?"

"Danger?" The president shook his head. "We don't know what you mean!"

Relieved, but still mystified, York recounted briefly the episode in space.

The president shook his head sadly.

"So that was the ultimate fate of those two!" he murmured, and went on in explanation. "They were two flyers who told a wild story. They claimed they had been to Mount Olympus and had found the mythological gods of Greece, or at least three of them, called the Three Eternals. Furthermore, they were evil beings and planned destruction of civilization, by causing some harebrained geological upheaval.

"They were so insistent that we sent ships to Mount Olympus, but of course nothing was found there. They claimed to have been in a great marble building. Obviously insane, they were sent to an asylum. They escaped three months ago, and we heard no more of them till today, from you. Their mad flight to Alpha Centauri to search for worlds to migrate to, proves their insanity. They insisted the three evil gods would not rest till all mankind were annihilated!"

Chapter 3

It was a strange story the councilor in Sol City related, and later, when York recounted it to Vera, he was still thoughtful.

"Hallucination, after all!" Vera said with a note of finality. "But, Tony, you still look a little worried."

"I am," he admitted. "What do you say, Vera, that we take a trip around this Forty-first Century world, just to see that everything is all right?"

Vera nodded enthusiastically.

"Let's! After a thousand years of absence, it will be intriguing to look over this old Earth of ours."

In their space ship, upheld and motivated by the subtle warpings of gravitation, they soared over the world of mortal men.

Civilization had taken great strides forward, particularly in technology and industry. All the great cities of the Thirty-first Century had grown greater still. The somewhat makeshift space ship dromes of that earlier time in interplanetary expansion had been replaced by magnificent structures. With remarkable speed and efficiency, ships could be unloaded, restocked, refueled and overhauled. Interplanetary trade flourished.

The population of this age had reached a new peak. No less than ten billion human beings scurried over Earth's surface, and at least another billion were spread among the other planets.

The food problem had been solved by weather control, the manufacture of artificial staples from mineral matter, and the conversion of all desert lands into vast gardens. The great Sahara was no longer a desert, as York and his wife had known it. Irrigation through a tremendous canal from the Mediterranean had transformed it into one giant wheat field.

To supply his ever-growing demand for metals, mankind had finally tapped the vast ocean reservoir. Hundreds of electrical plants, on important coasts, powered by the eternal tides, extracted salt products. Ocean water poured in one end, to come out at the other almost chemically pure. Every element known, in varying amounts, then reposed in the caked residues in their plants. It was simply a matter of the application of Forty-first Century chemistry to separate these materials.

The wealth of products thus made available could not be measured in antiquated terms of dollars and cents. Of radium alone, least abundant of the ocean solutes, there was extracted a full ton each year. Gold, now a useful metal for its resistance to corrosion, coated everything metallic that people wore or used daily.

The high economic standard resulting from this material wealth had also allowed cultural expansion. Even the most backward of races and groups had access to literature, art, music and facilities for scientific research. Travel was within the means of most, and the preserved wilds of central South America, North America's West, and parts of Asia and Africa were constantly frequented by tourists.

"And this is the civilization supposedly marked for destruction!" York mused. "Who would even contemplate such a thing? Who would have the power? I'm just about convinced, now, that those two poor devils were hopelessly insane." He brightened. "Now we can take another trip around the world, and really enjoy it!"

It was while they were leisurely crossing the South Atlantic one day that York suddenly halted their slow passage and lowered the ship toward water. In the bright sunlight, the smoothly rolling waves made a fascinating picture. But York stared as though he had never seen such a sight before. Finally he took out a pair of binoculars and trained them below.

"That's water, Tony!" laughed Vera. "Dihydrogen oxide—remember?"

"But you never saw water quite like that before," returned York seriously. "Look for yourself."

After a moment, Vera looked up from the glasses.

"Why, it looks as if countless little seeds are floating—"

"Those aren't seeds, but bubbles!" interposed York. "Millions upon millions of tiny bubbles coming up from the ocean floor. Let's find out how far their range is."

He was already at the controls, sending the ship parallel to the ocean level. A mile away he stopped, looked, nodded. "Still there!"

A mile further he went, again nodded. Next time he went five miles, then ten, a hundred, a thousand, and still found bubbles. His face grew solemn.

The next day he sent their ship scudding in straight lines north and south, and east and west, and in six other radial directions over the South Atlantic. He stopped every hundred miles while Vera reported with the binoculars. They mapped the area infused with bubbles as roughly three thousand miles long and two thousand miles wide, set squarely between Central America and Africa. It included all the Sargasso Sea.

"What does it mean?" asked Vera when her patience at her husband's moody silence had run out. "Why should this vast area of ocean surface be filled with bubbles? Where do they come from?"

"They can only come from below, from—" York paused, snapped on his radio. "Anton York calling the central radio exchange," he barked.

"Y-yes sir," came a half-frightened voice a moment later, awed by the distinguished caller. "What is it, sir?"

"Connect me with your main oceanology station in the Atlantic, please."

When the station at Cape Verde had answered and the director was called, York queried him.

"Yes," came the reply, "we've noticed those bubbles all right. They've been coming up for the past ten years! Their origin is beyond our best guesses. We've sent diving bells down a mile, our limit, without any clue. The bubbles must come from below that."

"One more question," York said. "Have the coast lines of the Atlantic changed at all in those ten years?"

Suddenly a sharp note of worry sprang into the director's voice.

"Yes! It's a disturbing fact that the entire coast line of western Europe is sinking at an unprecedented rate. Already, relatively, the water level has climbed a foot. Many coast lands will soon be threatened by inundation.

"The effect isn't local, however. The coasts of America are lowering also. And in the Pacific, the same thing is happening. There, too, a vast area of bubbles exists. We scientists have taken up the problem seriously. We don't know what this may lead to, if it keeps up, but we are making plans to dyke all sea coasts."

"Thanks."

York snapped off the radio abruptly. He stared unseeingly out of a port.

"If this keeps up," he murmured, "dykes won't help a bit. Coasts sinking! Is it a natural event—or otherwise!"

Vera looked at him queerly.

"Of course it's a natural event, Tony," she commented. "The gods of Fate play strange tricks. Perhaps Jove, dissatisfied with the present civilization, is trying to destroy it with Neptune's weapons. That's just the way myths grow, Tony, trying to explain—"

She stopped and gasped as her husband suddenly whirled, snapped his fingers, and dived for the pilot board as though their lives depended on it.

"Tony, have you gone crazy?"

"No, but I could kick myself!"

York sent the ship scuttling at the highest rate of speed safe in an atmosphere. His direction was east.

"I bow again to feminine intuition," he resumed. "We're going to Mount Olympus, Vera, to visit the gods! There's just a chance that those two lost souls were not mad. They did predict a geological upheaval. And then that man's dying words—"

"About the Three Eternals, Mount Olympus?" Vera cried. "Then Tony, maybe there's danger!"

But York did not answer. His face was set with a glowing anticipation as he drove for what he hoped would be the solution to a mystery as great as any he had ever encountered.

The globular ship raced over the southern coasts of Europe, over the Mediterranean, past what had formerly been Spain, France, Italy and Albania. It turned south a little into the mountainous interior of Greece. Finally the misty summit of Mount Olympus loomed ahead.

"Do you really expect to find something here?" asked Vera as they approached. "After all, it's just a Greek myth, dating from five thousand years ago, about Jove and the other gods."

York smiled peculiarly.

"Vera, we are myths too, a few centuries after each visit to Earth!"

Presently they were floating over the peak of Mount Olympus. They gazed down searchingly. As with other mountain tops, it was a scene of jagged rocks, scraggly growths, and dark hollows here and there tufted with snow.

"I hardly know what to look for, but nothing is there out of the ordinary," said Vera, almost in relief. "Besides, the president of the council said they had searched and found nothing."

"Look!" York pointed. "That large hollow to the left. Notice the shimmer over it?" He trained his periscope screen. "Can't clarify it. It looks almost as though—something is behind that shimmering mist!"

Vera grasped his arm. "Please, Tony, be careful!"

He lowered the ship cautiously until it was no more than a hundred yards over the strange, quiescent mist that did not stir in the wind. Still nothing could be distinguished beyond it save vague shadows and lights. Switching on his electro-protective screen, out of caution, York descended slowly till he had almost touched the layer of concealment.

A few more feet the ship sank, then stopped abruptly.

York and Vera looked at each other. No tangible barrier opposed them; only the queer, glittering, impenetrable mist. Experimentally, York put more power into his engine. His ship pressed against the weird obstruction until the hull creaked, but not one more inch was gained.

York eased up, muttering.

Then, with a suddenness that made them start, a powerful telepathic voice beat into their brains.

"Who is it seeks the presence of the Eternal Three?"

Glancing significantly at Vera, York answered, by the telepathy he had developed and used so many times before in space.

"Anton York, the Immortal!"

"Descend!"

Coincident with the word, the shimmering mist beneath their ship's keel vanished. Below was revealed the full extent of the hollow, desolate save for a huge marble building in its center. It was of ancient Grecian style, and the stone was stained with great age.

"Those two men were here!" gasped Vera. "They told the truth. Tony, do you suppose everything else they said—"

York shook his head non-committally.

Chapter 4

Anton York landed the ship before the edifice, leaving his electro-screen on. When the telepathic voice invited him to step into the building, York politely declined. Instead he snapped on his televisor requesting them to do the same, if they had such an instrument.

A moment later it proved they had and his screen became spangled with whirling lights that finally crystallized into the image of an ornately furnished room in which sat three men.

York and Vera looked at them closely.

Their rich, velvety togas were of a strange, unknown style. Their features, though strictly human, were a strange blend of Oriental and Nordic qualities. In age, they all seemed at the prime of life. But most of all it was noticeable that their eyes glowed with that same strange light that was in York's and Vera's—the sign of immortality!

"We have been expecting you, Anton York," said one of the three, still using the universal language of telepathy. "Ever since your arrival in the Solar System, we knew you would hear of us. How did it happen?"

York told of meeting the derelict ship, and the resurrected man's words.

"He said you had threatened destruction of civilization!" he concluded challengingly.

The spokesman smiled frostily.

"Yes, I believe we did tell them the story. Briefly, some months ago, they were flying over Mount Olympus in an airplane. Its motors failed and they smashed up on our roof of protective mist. As a whim, we nursed their lives. As a further whim, we told him the story you heard. We wanted to see if it would drive them mad. But we lost interest in them quickly, sent them away. We have lived a long, long time. Nothing in the world of mortals interests us any more."

Something of rage arose in York at the calm, cold way the man spoke of other humans.

"You had no right to toy with two human lives!" he cried hotly.

The Eternal shrugged.

"We have lived a long, long time," he repeated. "Conceptions of right and wrong melt into one another through the centuries."

York was about to reply angrily again when Vera touched his arm.

"Don't argue with them, Tony—no use!" she whispered rapidly, consciously willing her broadcast thoughts blank. "Find out all you can about them instead."

York pressed her hand, spoke to the trio of cold-faced men.

"Just how long have you lived?"

Again the icy, disdainful smiles from all three of them.

"You have lived how long, Anton York—some two thousand years since you were inoculated with the radiogen-renewing serum? We, too, were given such an elixir of youth to keep up eternally at our prime, but that was—twenty thousand years ago!"

The incredible statement left both York and Vera numb for a moment. These three had lived for almost an astronomical age!

"It can't be true!" stammered Vera. "It can't."

"It is true, however," assured the Eternals. "For twenty thousand years we three have lived and breathed. You wonder how we could have filled in our time. Most of it has been spent in space, as you two have spent your time. We have roamed endless distances, seen uncounted other worlds of other suns.

"However, at first it intrigued us to do certain things in the Solar System. We laughed to ourselves, Anton York, when we saw you moving asteroids and giving Jupiter rings. For you were simply carrying on what we had dropped in boredom. We were the ones who made Saturn's rings! And we had blown up the planet revolving between Mars and Jupiter, testing our powers, to make the present day asteroids.

"Venus originally had a moon which we moved to a new orbit. It is called Mercury now. Mercury, in mythology, is the wandering god—or the wandering planet. We named all the planets.

"But these things lost their novelty after a time. We did no more. Wandering through the void and observing other worlds and civilizations occupied much more of our time. That eventually palled also. Immortality has its penalty of ennui, as you will notice, too, when you have lived a little longer and seen the ashes of futility behind the fires of life.

"In the past five thousand years we have stayed on Earth, finding its pageantry at least interesting as anything else in the Universe. We have been in mankind's history, even as you have been. We, not the primitive Egyptians, built the great Cheops Pyramid, though they copied it with theirs. It is our marker to show the slow passing of time in a swifter scale. Each century the light of a fixed star moves a little along the scale at the back of a passageway. 'Fixed' star! Even the stars have moved, in our time!

"We caused the Noachin Flood, inadvertently, when we split once solid Gibraltar, filling the Mediterranean basin. For a time, during the great Grecian Era, we mingled somewhat with mortals, giving rise to their famous mythology. Our science deeds and seeming miracles, in various roles, impressed them as the doings of a race of gods.

"And other things we have done. But these things, too, have ceased to interest us. In the past three thousand years we have done little but sigh and wonder if perhaps suicide would not be preferable to the slow poison of ennui. Even your rise two thousand years ago, Anton York, and your exploits of a thousand years ago, failed to intrigue us more than casually. We have utterly lost that strange but important human ability to care about anything!"

Suddenly York and Vera saw in their eyes the haunting lassitude of spirit that obsessed them. They were three incredibly old men—despite their young bodies—who had tasted life to the full and could no longer wring out one drop of stimulation. Mentally, they had already died.

Anton York drew a long breath. At times he, too, even in his comparatively short two thousand years of existence, had wondered how long it would be before there would be nothing new to him—nothing further to lure his interest. Then he shook off the dull spell. One must not think of such things too much.

"From what land do you come, preceding recorded human history?" he asked, anticipating the answer.

"Atlantis," was the reply from the Three Eternals. "At that time Atlantis in the Atlantic Ocean and Lemuria in the Pacific were two great continents. Their civilizations touched heights never since exceeded. But they warred incessantly, and it was to lead to their mutual destruction.

"We three had been great scientists of that time. We discovered the secret of immortality, partook of it. Also conquering gravity, as did you, we went out into space for a time. When we came back, Atlantis and Mu lay under the oceans, and new lands had risen! Atlantis, in trying to undermine Mu with giant atomic-power machines, touched off a fault in Earth's crust, leading to world-wide holocaust.

"Thus, we three found ourselves orphaned from the world we had known. Our magnificent cities and glorious monuments lay under the ocean ooze. Strangely, that is the only thing that can now stir our hearts—thought of that ancient glory. A nostalgia that has survived twenty thousand years—and has grown stronger!"

York's nerves became tense.

"Yes?" he prompted.

A slight glow came into their faces as their spokesman went on. His psychic voice vibrated strongly.

"Thus we have decided to bring up our homeland of Atlantis, from its briny grave. Resurrect it, rehabilitate it, restore some semblance of its former grandeur. A long, tedious task, perhaps, but one we will truly enjoy." A fanatic light came into his eyes. "Sentimentality is the one human emotion we have not lost. We cherish a memory. It can be molded into reality. Atlantis must rise again!"

York and his wife looked at one another. That accounted for the bubbles over the South Atlantic. The ocean floor ooze, disturbed after long ages of quiescence, was giving up its occluded gases.

"How is it being done?" queried York, feigning deep curiosity, and nothing more.

"It is simple. We made a long study of Earth's crust, through seismological data. Any major geologic disturbance is linked to others. They form a chain. By setting them off in the proper order, any desired end result can be obtained. Exploding a certain small island in the Atlantic, we started waves of concussion in the thin, unstable crust. The slow, irresistible forces existing in the plastic layer beneath the crust were awakened. They will culminate by pushing the floor of the Atlantic and Pacific up above water level.

"This was started ten years ago. Perhaps in another century or so, the process will be completed. We are in no hurry. Then we will begin our great reconstruction of Atlantean glory!"

"Can the process be stopped?" asked York, wondering if they would answer.

It may have been a mocking light that shone from their eyes as the reply came.

"Yes, by a suitable counter wave in the crust, to neutralize the first."

York snapped himself alert. He had heard all he wanted to hear. His telepathic radiations almost crackled as he said:

"And in the meantime, Earth's billions of people will go to their doom!"

"That is unfortunate." The Eternal shrugged. "However, some few will be chosen and saved to repopulate the new Atlantis. The rest must die simply because they will have no place in our new world. All the old lands will not sink, but for a time, as the process approaches its climax, there will be violent earthquakes and storms that will decimate most of them."

"It's the most cold-blooded scheme ever thought of by man!" raged York, his self-control breaking. "You must not go on with it!"

The Three Eternals in the visi-screen looked annoyed, then faintly amused.

"Who will stop us? You?"

"Yes!" returned York grimly. "I give you fair warning. I have a weapon whose activity you have probably seen wielded. In ten seconds, if you do not agree to reverse your geological process, I'll use it!"

"You are brave, Anton York, but foolishly so," the answer came back imperturbably. "We have illimitable power, we three."

"One!" interposed York, in answer.

With his protective screen on full power, York trained his weapon's snout at the marble building and counted tensely. The Eternal triumvirate sat there disdainfully, as though unaware of danger. One of them idly reached over to a panel and flipped a small switch. York's clammy finger tightened at the count of nine, squeezed at ten.

The ravening burst of energy that sprang from his gun expended itself harmlessly against an invisible screen surrounding the marble temple. Beyond it, rocks and trees shriveled into a soot-black mist that drifted upward like vagrant smoke. The weapon's force was that of subgamma and ultra-sound waves, able to shatter molecules to black shreds.

York desperately rammed on full power, never before used, and left it for a full minute. The opposing screen did not weaken in the slightest. York gasped. Even his own screen, he knew, would not have withstood that hell fury for that long. The Three Eternals, in the visi-screen, smiled scoffingly.

Sensing his own danger, York leaped for the controls. But at the same moment, some paralyzing force gripped his body, held him rigid. One of the Eternals was manipulating controls on his panel.

"Rash one!" came the telepathic taunt. "We have more command of natural forces that you could dream of! We are masters of twenty thousand years of science. Anton York, you have declared war on us. We should annihilate you on the spot, as we could easily do. But it would be beneath our dignity to destroy that which cannot harm us. Therefore, go with your life. But never again test our patience and strength!"

Anton York's ship eased off the ground, in the grip of some intangible force. Suddenly it was flung upward, as though by a Titan's hand. York and Vera were thrown into a heap in a corner of their cabin, but the paralysis left them. York grasped a hand-rail, half dragged himself toward the pilot board and quickly righted the ship. Then he helped Vera to her feet.

York said nothing but his face burned with humiliation. They had been cast away as though they had been vermin. He looked down as the ship floated at even keel. The shimmering mist lay over the hollow, hiding its three eternal inhabitants. Hiding a menace supreme!

York knew it was no use to continue aggression openly. His gamma-sonic weapon—never before unsuccessful—had failed to pierce the defense of the Three Immortals. Even the furies of atomic power were a lesser force. The Three were impregnable. If York was a god in his powers, they were super-gods.

"What can we do against them?" wailed Vera. "Against twenty thousand years of science?"

York sent his ship away from Mount Olympus. He did not attempt to answer a question that had no immediate answer. But a bleak look had come into his eyes—the reflection of a super-mind wrestling with a super-problem.

Chapter 5

During the next year, the crews and passengers of various ocean liners and huge transoceanic aircraft sighted York's globular ship, here and there. At times it hovered motionlessly over water. At other times over islands. Several times it was seen at the docks of Sol City, picking up certain apparatus that the council had had manufactured at York's orders. No one knew, not even the councilors, what the instruments were for.

Inside the ship, York labored as only a man with a set idea can work. The instruments were ultra-divining rods. By an intricate sonic principle, they were able to make clear the structure of inner Earth, as the X-ray reveals a skeleton. York could send down a sound wave that would reflect, hours later, from the hot core of Earth.

York finally accumulated a sheaf of papers scrawled with condensed mathematical equations and notes. Salted throughout the manuscript were dynamical formulae involving mountain-sized masses of land, water and air. Trembling, he fingered the pages.

"No time to make them look pretty," he murmured to Vera. "But I have it almost completely worked out. With my seismological observations of the past year to go by, the Earth as a whole has been moved into the laboratory. I have dealt with this planet as though it were a compound in a test tube, or a slide under a microscope. With these Earth dynamics, I can predict the result of any major geological phenomenon, just as the Three Eternals worked it out. Look!"

He spread out a large flat map of the world and put his pencil tip on a spot in the Atlantic Ocean.

"An island existed here ten years ago. The Three Eternals knew it to be the key to their aim. They exploded it. The tremendous ground waves this started touched off certain strains in Earth's crust. Atlantis and Mu, long buried, began rising. The other lands are slowly sinking. But I can stop it!" York's pencil moved to the Pacific, circling a dozen tiny atolls among the Polynesian group.

"The key lies somewhere here," he explained. "The antidote to their poison. The explosion of one of these islands will send out ground waves setting off related, but opposing strains. There will be a cancellation of effects. In a decade or less, Earth will quiet down with no more than a few coasts undermined. Atlantis and Mu will not rise!"

"All humanity, now and in the future, will owe you its life!" cried Vera, happy in his success. Suddenly a deep horror flooded her eyes. "But the Three Eternals will destroy you—us—for it, Tony! What is to prevent them? Can they destroy us, Tony, or—"

To Vera it was a strange thought that anyone or anything could destroy them. For had they not lived two thousand years?

York nodded somberly. "They can!" He clamped his teeth together firmly. "But first we'll finish our job, and then think of that. I still have to determine exactly which island to demolish."

A few hours later their ship hovered over Southern Pacific waters. Only a few uninhabited islands speckled the vast reaches of ocean. York carried on his sub-surface probings, but finally gave a baffled grunt.

"I've narrowed the field down to three of these islands," he mused, "but I can't seem to go any further with the data, from here. I have to be dead sure I explode the right island. If I hit the wrong one, the result might be just as catastrophic as what the Three Eternals started."

He thought a moment. "Vera, there's only one way. These measurements involve the strains *within* Earth's crust. I must map the strains at first hand. I must go down there, in person. Down miles and miles below the ocean, to where the greater ocean of subsea plasma fumes." His brow wrinkled thoughtfully, as the mind behind already began shaping a machine unknown to Earthly science. "No mines or man-made submarines go down that far, of course. I'll have an Earth-boring ship made—a mechanical mole. I'll—"

Vera was quick to sense something in her husband's words.

"You're using too many 'I's' Tony. You're not going down without me!"

"It's liable to be very dangerous, Vera. World-shattering forces lie down there." Seeing the set of her jaw, he tried a humorous tack. "Why don't you visit your aunt for a few weeks?"

But instead of smiling, her eyes became a little sad. She had no aunt, or relatives at all from that long-gone day of their birth. Neither had York.

"We even have no descendants," she murmured, for that had been the price of immortality. "No one on this Earth we can remotely call kin. Tony, don't you see? If I stayed up here and you, going below, never came back, I'd be more lonely than the loneliest meteor in space!"

Within another year, the precision factories of the Forty-first Century industry had turned out the parts from York's blue-prints. Time, of which they had a plethora, meant nothing to the eternal pair as they superintended the construction.

The mechanical mole took shape as a segmented cylinder of fused, transparent diamond—York's secret—buttressed with steel of colossal strength. Its front end held the fan-wise jets of York's gamma-sonic force, for converting solid matter to impalpable dust. The technicians who assembled the machine understood little of what they made, further than that it could possibly plow through anything short of neutronium.

The completed vehicle was shipped to one of the Polynesian Islands, via barge dragged by the world's largest freight ship, and here York dismissed all attendants. Alone with Vera, he drew a breath.

"I've been wondering all this time if the Three Eternals would find out and interfere in some way," he confided, "despite the secrecy with which it was done."

Vera shuddered, as she always did at mention of the Three.

"They're like three vultures, waiting, waiting—"

York waved a hand. "Take a last look at the Sun, dear. We may not see it again for weeks!"

Then he led the way into the craft, sealing its pneumatic hatch. An hour later, after carefully checking the supplies of tanked air, food, water, and his many instruments, he started the motor.

The titanic energies of gravity warped into his coils, spraying disintegrative forces from the under nose jets. The nose of the ship dived into the pit formed and like a great worm, it bored downward, roaring powerfully. In seconds, the segmented tail of the ship had vanished beneath the surface. When it had penetrated through top soil and loose ground, it struck bed-rock and there the rate of boring settled to an average of eight hundred feet an hour.

Swirls of black soot shot back from the rock-eating nose, so that they saw little of their course into Earth's skin. It was a bumpy ride, and vibration shook them so violently that they clamped their teeth tight to keep them from rattling like castanets. Each hour York stopped the ship and let their aching bodies recuperate somewhat.

Down and down the mechanical mole drilled, meeting no material obstacle that its blasting rays could not whiff to unresisting dust. Once their rate slowed by half, as they went through a hard-grained granitic stratum, packed densely by the crushing weight overhead.

York did not fear collapse of the tunnel about them. The braced diamond-walls of the ship would have survived the weight of Mount Everest, balanced on its tip, on each square inch of surface.

A week later, York stopped the ship when his gravity instruments read twenty-five miles below Earth's sea level. For three days he and Vera rested their bruised bodies and jangled nerves.

"Well," said York then, "here we are, twenty-five miles down, deeper than man has ever been before within the Earth he lives upon like"—he thought of an appropriate metaphor—"like bacteria swarming about a marble."

With Vera's skilled help, York made tests of temperature, pressure, density of the solid rock about them, with instruments that extended out of walled pockets in the hull. Most important of all, he measured the strain imposed by the mighty masses of rock above, and the pressing hot core of Earth below. The figures represented leashed forces whose unbinding would have buckled Earth's crust like a toasted apple skin.

"They are ordinarily in balance, these brute forces," said York. "The Three Eternals have unsettled them to the extent of raising two continents and lowering the rest. We have to restore the balance."

A week later, he again started the motor and drilled downward.

"My answer doesn't lie here," he decided. "We'll have to penetrate almost fifty miles down, right through the crust to the barysphere. It is semifluid and hot. We'll have to be very careful."

Vera knew without saying that they were risking their lives. But so they had many times before, out in space. They were calm in the thought that if they went, they would go together. York was glad now that Vera had insisted on coming along.

At a depth under Earth of forty-five miles, York again halted. Strangely, the temperature was not much greater here than it had been at twenty-five miles. In fact, not much more than man's deepest mines.

"Earth's skin is a good conductor of heat," York explained for his own satisfaction. "And brings most of it directly to the surface, which accounts for volcanic action, hot springs, and the non-freezing of the sunless ocean bottoms."

Slowly he dictated a mass of measurement data to Vera, using his instruments. Hourly, he became more excited. Finally, a day later, he was jubilant.

"I have it now, Vera!" he cried. "The plasma stresses have a node, a point of concentration, right here! It runs as a straight line up to the island next to the one we bored down into. When we destroy that island, counter waves in the crust will cancel those started by the Three Eternals and then—"

"Tony!" It was a sharp cry from Vera. "Tony, I feel strange! I feel as though someone were near us—telepathy—"

"Nonsense!" snapped York, slightly annoyed. "Who could be forty-five miles under the surface?" He started. "Except the Three—"

"Eternal Three!" came the distinct telepathic message, mockingly.

And at that moment, one entire side of the tunnel in which their ship rested dissolved away. A craft lay revealed beyond. It was segmented, like theirs, but larger and with a hull of some clear, greenish material through which were plainly visible the three leadenly-calm, almost unhuman features of the three dwellers of Mount Olympus!

Chapter 6

York felt the alarmed pumping of Vera's heart, her body pressed against his, and his own pulse raced. Fool, that he hadn't thought of bringing down a weapon with him! But even that, he reflected with sagging spirit, would not have helped, against the impregnable Three.

"Anton York," came the telepathic voice, heavy with threat from the other Earth-boring ship, "you have signed your own death warrant. We have been picking up your conscious thoughts, with certain long-range psychic instruments, ever since you left us, at Mount Olympus. We detected that you were trying to upset our plans. We did not think you would succeed in finding the necessary data. But when you dived underneath the Earth, we followed in the mechanical mole ship we used for our measurements twelve years ago. As a scientist you are seemingly a little more adept than we thought."

The Eternals paused as though to give the ironic compliment full play.

"So adept that we must now destroy you. There cannot be two masters of Earth!"

"I do not wish to master Earth!" remonstrated York. "Only save it!" He tried pleading. "Think once, what you are doing—murdering ten billion people! Even if you live to the end of eternity, your conscience could never be free of that stigma!"

"You are an idealist, Anton York," responded the implacable trio. "We are realists. The present race and civilization do not deserve continuance. They are cluttered with traditions, superstitions, periodic setbacks of their own devising. Scarcely three centuries ago, there was again a worldwide 'depression,' accompanied by needless famine, rioting and maladjustment of affairs. Civilization fell back as it has so many times."

"But it climbs steadily!" reminded York.

"When we have raised Atlantis and Mu," the voice went on, ignoring his remark, "we will people them with a new race, set in a super-civilization, like a precious stone glittering in a setting of purest gold."

"And in ten years there will be bickering, struggle for power, and anarchy," predicted York quickly. "You are the idealists, so divorced from your former life that you do not realize the fundamental rule of life—experience! Your new civilization, started at the topmost stage, would collapse into the hollow sands of its non-existent foundations."

For the first time, a trace of anger came from the Eternals, as though their pride had been pricked by this calm, searching analysis.

"Cease, fool! You are to die. But one thing we wish to learn from you before you go—the secret of your gamma-sonic weapon. Though it did not destroy us, and though we have equal forces, we wish to add it to our knowledge. Speak!"

York's silence was stinging.

"Very well," resumed the Eternals' spokesman. "We will get it anyway. In advance, knowing your nature, we've planned how. You will be left to die, in this cavern, without your ship. Without a single implement with which to dig—or commit suicide. You will go insane, before death by asphyxiation. In that condition, your mind will automatically throw off all its thoughts, willed and unwilled. Back in our laboratory at Mount Olympus, an instrument is set to pick up the mental record, and at our leisure we will extract from it the gamma-sonic data. Thus you will die and serve us at the same time."

There was no fiendish note in the quiet exposition of their hideous plan. It was a cold, passionless scheme, in which human feeling meant nothing. York doubted that they knew the meaning of love, anger, hate, mercy, or any emotion. Twenty thousand years of living had drained them dry of all but crystallized intellect.

A few minutes later, York and Vera stood alone in the cavern that had been formed by the two mechanical moles. Their ship was gone, disintegrated before their eyes by a cold beam which caused matter to fall into rotting grains. York and Vera had previously been carried out of the ship, under the

Eternals' paralysis ray. Then the Three had released one tank of oxygen into the space, lest they die too soon. Finally, their ship had left, spraying a heat ray behind it that fused its own trail, as the Eternals had fused off the tunnel made by York's ship.

"This is our end, Tony!" whispered Vera, huddling close to him. "Dying like trapped rats, forty-five miles under Earth's surface, in a sealed pocket of rock. But we'll fool them, Tony, in one thing. We won't go insane. We'll talk over our life—two thousand years of it. It's been glorious. We'll die in peace!"

York kissed her tenderly for her bravery and they talked. They renewed stirring memories of their sojourn in space, and of their last two visitations to Earth. But within an hour their voices faltered and their nerves shrieked.

They could see each other by weird radio-active glow from the surrounding rock. It was more hellish than darkness would have been. Aching silence greeted every pause in their speech. The excessive warmth began to torture their bodies, unrelieved by a breath of current in the confined air.

They were buried alive! That corrosive thought ate into their enforced resignation.

Vera began to babble aimlessly, her eyes wild. York fought back the darkening cloud of madness. Was there no escape? They had no slightest tool, implement, or material object other than their clothing and their bodies.

No escape! They had not even a spoon with which to start digging, useless as that would have been with forty-five miles of stone to penetrate. York had the inane thought for a moment that they had fingernails, something to scratch with—madness!

"One thing I have," he remembered, without the slightest surge of hope. "The brain-wave instrument within my left ear, with which I commanded the councilors. The Three Eternals missed it, or disdained it. But what good is it? I can command minds with it, but stone is mindless."

And soon they, too, would be as mindless as their imprisoning walls.

"I can hear your thoughts," Vera mumbled, laughing hysterically. "You won't give up, Tony, but how foolish. You're trying to think a way out— think a way out—think a way out—"

Her voice began to repeat like a cracked phonograph record, as her mind teetered.

"Think a way out!" echoed York, his mind clicking. Suddenly he grabbed Vera, shaking her violently. "Vera, maybe that's it! My brain-wave concentrator projects telekinetic forces. With it, I made other minds cause their bodies to act, move. Perhaps, without the relay minds between, I can use telekinesis to make movement—even of stone!"

"Move stone?" Vera said sepulchrally, in a moment of calm. "But that would take energy, much more than to cause mobile human machines to move, as with the councilors. Energy, lots of it, to move tons of stone over which are tons more—" Her voice broke. "Tony, why do we even think of it? False hopes are just added torture."

"Energy," mumbled York defeatedly. "More energy than our bodies contain, if we could use even that."

He ground the thought of telekinesis out of his mind and joined in Vera's resignation.

"Die in peace—we must," Vera murmured, straining against another attack of hysteria.

"It's a little ironic, isn't it?" mused York. "Two thousand years of science at my fingertips, gathered in thirty lifetimes of thought and research. And yet, without tools, I'm as helpless as any single-lived man would be, in this same dilemma. A thousand years ago, in a great ship, I moved planets. Today, stripped of implements, I'm no better than a worm."

Something probed into his mind. He had felt it many times before in the past years, without realizing it had been the Three Eternals, spying out his thoughts.

"Still sane?" came the cold, blunt psychic voice of one of the Eternals, rather faintly. "You have remarkable fortitude, Anton York. But you will succumb, even as we might, be it admitted. We are halfway to the surface. When we reach it, you will be babbling, spilling your mind into our recorders." The voice clicked off.

Vera shrieked. She had heard too.

"Don't, Vera!" soothed York. "Don't you see? They did that to drive us to insanity more quickly. Let's remember our resolve—to die in peace."

"If we only could!" she moaned. "But it's such torture. And my skin, itching—that radioactive emanation—"

York felt it too, a bothersome tingling on his skin, to add to their discomfort. It was caused by radium in the rock.

York leaped up.

"Radium—energy!" he cried. "Energy for the telekinesis! There it is, all around us! Vera, I'm going to try it. My brain wave should be able to utilize this energy as well as that of a human body."

He offered up a prayer to all the gods in the Universe that he was right.

Vera, sobered by hope, watched him. York stood, facing one wall, his face drawn into a pucker of fierce concentration. The same intangible force with which he had impelled the councilors to sit down and listen to him now sprang against the rock. York had never fully tested the mental ray's possibilities. Could he command matter to fall away before him?

New beads of sweat joined those from the heat, on his brow. Nothing visible, nothing of which he even knew the formula, hurtled against adamant rock. Radioactive energy lay pulsing there. Could he tap it, mold it to his use, with nothing more than pure mentality?

Aching minutes passed. Then slowly the rock began to slough away into a depression. There was a rustle, as of billions of crystals rubbing against one another, changing position.

Matter obediently aligned itself in a circular wall, forming a tunnel.

York walked forward, step by step, like a god before whom nothing could stand. Foot by foot, the tunnel shaped itself.

"Follow me!" York said to Vera, in clipped phrases, without turning his head. "It's working—mind over matter—telekinesis, energized by radium."

York fashioned his mind-wrought tunnel on the steepest upgrade they could climb. It was no use to bore to the ship's tunnel, as that rose almost perpendicularly. He would have to push on at a slant, through perhaps a hundred miles of rock, before reaching the Sun. A problem arose—that of thinning air, as the tunnel extended. York stopped to command oxygen to spring out of the rock. It did, in gusty abundance.

"Chemical telekinesis!" he said to Vera. "Even the electrons and protons shape new atoms, under this mental force. Vera, this is a true miracle of science!"

He went on, shaping his tunnel. The lack of radium in certain strata, later, did not stop York, for his mind had subtly found the way to extract even the locked energy in non-radioactive rock. In foresight, he made the tunnel oval-shaped, distributing the tremendous pressures in the rock around Nature's sturdiest geometrical design. The unbolstered cavern held, for the same reason that a fragile-shelled egg can resist terrific pressure.

Back of them, a while later, they heard a sudden rumble, as their former prison space collapsed. York stopped, facing Vera.

"Quick!" he said, in inspiration. "Will your broadcast thoughts blank. Let the Three Eternals think we died!"

For an hour they remained quiet. They could feel the strange mental probe darting about their closed minds—the Three Eternals trying to discover some mental sign of life from their recent prisoners. York cautioned Vera to hold out, even when the tunnel back of them progressively collapsed.

At last the psychic finger left. The Eternals were convinced of their deaths!

Chapter 7

Hopeful now of true escape, York forged ahead. His mental chisel, powered by mighty demons of energy, forced the creaking, groaning rock aside, against blind, brute gravity. When his mind began to reel, drained of energy, he transferred his brain wave concentrator into Vera's ear. Her progress in forming the tunnel was little slower than his.

Later, when food and water became necessity, York commanded these. Water dripped from the rock overhead, into their mouths. Food, though a more stubborn problem, was solved when York dug up from memory the exact chemical formulae of starches, proteins and sugars, which he had determined as an esoteric research, centuries before. At command, the pliant rock molecules gathered into globules of these nutritious compounds and fell into their hands.

"It's so incredible!" murmured Vera, munching, as though unable to believe all this had happened.

"The tool of mentality!" responded York. "I've hit upon it by accident. It is probably the ultimate in forces, if it is fully developed."

Some hours later, when they had progressed miles, York almost fell forward on his face. His tunnel had broken through into a large chamber. They stepped forward and saw, in the weird glow of radioactive walls, a gigantic ovoid cavern, its walls and ceiling braced with ten-foot-square ribs of metal.

"Man-made!" whispered Vera in awe, her voice reverberating back in amplified echoes. She sniffed. "Breathable air, but musty. The place seems old—terribly old!"

"I think I know what this must be!" cried York, eyes lighting. "Remember the Three Eternals' story—Atlantis undermining Mu, in their war? This must have been an underground headquarters, from which the Atlantides drilled upward for their frightful task!"

Though they had seen many strange things, in the worlds of space, none struck them with more eerie wonder than this relic of an ancient folly on their own world.

Nothing remained in the chamber of twenty thousand years before save the metal ribbing which had withstood subterranean pressures for an age. Two great metal doors once leading the way in and out, still held, though by now masses of rock must press against them. The Atlantides had built well.

Yes, one thing remained, they saw. An enormous square block of metal squatted in the exact center of the floor, of no discernible purpose. York and Vera walked past it, on their way to start their new tunnel in the opposite wall.

Vera stopped abruptly, her face shocked. Slowly she turned this way and that, finally fastening her eyes on the metal block as though hypnotized.

"Tony, I heard a telepathic voice—from within this metal block!"

York, at first skeptical, turned back, knowing his wife was more sensitive to faint impulses than he was. Standing close to the side of the block, concentrating, they seemed to hear a dim voice. It was an inarticulate psychic mumble, exactly as though some one were day-dreaming.

"Someone is in there!" gasped York, walking around the block to find it solid metal on all sides, and at the top.

Finally he stood back, on straddled legs, and fixed his eyes on the metal. A depression formed, matter sloughed away, as his telekinetic beam ate inward. It was York, the scientist who did this, unable to pass by the mystery of a mind voice from within a metal block.

Suddenly there was no more reaction. His mental ray had struck something it could not penetrate, halfway in. Then they heard strange stirrings, and the psychic mumble clicked off. A dim form crept out of the opening York had made. Vera trembled and slipped her hand in his. What unbelievable Thing, imprisoned in metal, had survived—how long—and was coming out?

"A robot!" breathed York, when it stood clear.

It was obviously built in the image of man, but grotesquely disproportioned. Its body, though metallic-looking, seemed to be as flexible as rubber. Its faceless head bore two gleaming eye mirrors over which shutters blinked rapidly, as though even the dim glow of the cavern blinded it after total darkness.

It looked around slowly, with a queer air of bewilderment. Finally its eyes turned to them.

"No, not entirely a robot," it telepathized clearly, but haltingly. "I have a human brain within my skull-case. My name is Kaligor. Now tell me, what—what world is this?"

"Earth!" returned York, surprised. "What else could it be? You are from Atlantis, or perhaps Mu, Kaligor?"

"Atlantis? Mu?" The telepathic voice was uncertain. "Yes, Mu, of course. Now I remember! You must forgive my slowness. I have been buried in that block of metal for a long time—since the sinking of Atlantis and Mu. How long is that?"

"Twenty thousand years!" breathed York.

"Only twenty thousand years?" The man-robot seemed astonished. "I had thought it to be much longer—almost eternity!"

York and Vera looked at each other. Before, after only one hour, they had felt themselves going mad. How had this mind, human though metal-housed, survived two hundred centuries!

Kaligor caught their amazement.

"It is a long, queer story," he vouched. "I nearly did go mad, in the first few hours. Then I took hold of myself and saw that I could save sanity only by rigid mental discipline. There was only one answer—escape fantasies of my own devising. I must have some one thing, a complicated path, along which my thoughts could wind slowly. In those twenty thousand years I have devised, mentally, an entire new Universe! In a framework of six-dimensional geometry!"

He paused, then went on. "I meticulously thought out each separate sun, its weight, size, brilliance, spectrum, and so on. Finishing this, possibly within a century, I took one particular sun, pictured a mythical system of planets around it, and worked out all the elaborate details of their orbits, satellites, eclipses, and such. Still I found I must go on!"

"You hoped for rescue all that time!" cried York. "For twenty thousand years?"

Surely, in all eternity, there had never been a longer wait!

"I've been justified, haven't I?" returned the robot-mind, with grim lightness. "Since you stand before me, my rescuers! Ah, but how slow-footed was time! I dared not stop building my fantasy world. At that moment I would go insane, realizing my hopeless predicament. To get into greater detail, consuming more time, I peopled one of the worlds with intelligent beings, far different from humans. I devised their complete biological background, to the last cell.

"Sometimes, for what must have been days, I would wrestle with one single problem—for instance, the number of blood vessels in an inner organ. These intelligent beings, though their appearance would strike you with horror, are almost as real to me as you two now! In fact—"

He broke off, began again, his telepathic voice only now beginning to smooth its first halting pace.

"I had these imaginary beings—Wolkians, I called them—war with one another, explore their world, trade, and all the other activities of a busy civilization. But still time hung endlessly before me—perhaps all eternity! So I conjured up single characters, in my dream world, and followed their lives from birth to death. I sketched out thereafter dozens of individual histories in complete detail. Some of my creations I grew to hate; some to love. There was brave Mirbel, and lovely Binti, for whom he fought—"

Kaligor's psychic voice trailed away into an inarticulate mumble again. He started suddenly.

"But you would not understand," he resumed, "how real these children of my brain are to me. On and on I spun my formless dream, to keep that crushing thought of my rockbound prison, from my conscious thoughts. I have lived a thousand lives, adventures, dreams. I am even now half wondering if this may not be part of my dream!"

"No, this is real." York smiled, but at the same time realizing a character in Kaligor's dream might say the same thing.

And in that way had Kaligor kept from going mad.

He shook himself suddenly, as though throwing off the last shreds of his age-long dream.

"Who are you?" he asked. "How did you happen to come to this forgotten chamber?"

York told their story. At mention of the Three Eternals, Kaligor started and seemed to listen with rapt interest.

"The Three Eternals!" he burst out, when York had finished. "They are the same three who imprisoned me here! It came about in this way. I am of Mu, not Atlantis. I discovered the life-elixir, independently, partook of it, and in my utter zeal, decided to house my already immortal brain in an indestructible body, so that even accidental death could not claim my life. I would live forever! Ah, it was a foolish aim, not knowing at the time how palling life can become." For a moment Kaligor radiated the same ultra ennui of the Three Eternals. York and Vera realized that perhaps some day they too would long for escape.

Kaligor went on. "We had skilled surgeons in our civilization, and one of these I had transfer my living, immortal brain into this robot housing. I had previously devised a solution surrounding my brain that drew energy from space itself, which pervades all things. I had spent two centuries constructing my robot body. It is not metal, as it appears to your eye. It is not matter at all, for matter can be destroyed. I wanted something absolutely indestructible. This body of mine is made of—what shall I call it?—interwoven energy. A sort of fibroid cloth of fundamental warped space time. When you destroy an atom, what is left? Its energy, which cannot be destroyed—ever. Of this is my body made." York faintly understood. "I see why my brain wave stopped so suddenly when it struck your form. I was commanding pure energy to vanish, with pure energy. A figure telling its mirror image to begone!"

Kaligor waved a stumpy hand, in dismissal and went on. "Thus finally and truly immortal, I began to think of the future. Plans of leading Mu's civilization to astounding heights formed. And then, before I could begin, Mu crashed down into the sea, in that Titanic struggle for mastery with Atlantis, our bitter enemy.

"Tons of masonry fell on me, with no effect, of course. I found myself at the bottom of the sea, eventually, all my people drowned, murdered. Walking over the sea bottom to the shores of Atlantis, filled with horror, I was prepared to wreak vengeance. But Atlantis went down of itself, and civilization was done!"

His psychic tones were dull. "I must have sat on a mountain top, overlooking the broad seas that covered Mu, for a century, brooding, thinking I was the only human mind alive. But one day, in this newly arisen continent, I saw human forms. Some had survived! I questioned them. Though half savage, and the sinking of Mu and Atlantis already a legend to them, I found they were descendants of Muan survivors. My own people! My spirits sang and I began teaching them, building a new Muan civilization in place of the old."

He paused, his thoughts darkening. "Then the Three Eternals came. I met them for the first time. They had been in space, as they told you, and had come back to find their land and mine in limbo. Being Atlantides, they hated the thought of Muans inheriting the new world. We battled. I could not vanquish them, without weapons, nor could they destroy me, though they blasted me with every hellish force of their devising.

"At last, chaining me, they took me down to this chamber, buried me forty miles below Earth's surface in a solid, metal block, knowing that as long as Earth existed, I would live and think and never be free. Even insane, I could not die! Their last words to me were that they were going above to hunt down the Mu-descended savages. Every last one. Rather an Earth peopled only by dumb animals than Muans, was their bitter text."

"They obviously failed." York smiled grimly. "Since human life went on and civilization rose again, in time—Egypt, Sumeria, Maya, and so on."

Kaligor's bright mirror eyes looked at them strangely.

"And you, Anton York, are of my race. We have a bond between us, linking us across an age of time. And we have a common enemy,—the Three Eternals. You can see what their present plan means—to destroy once and for all the second Muan race and civilization. They will be forced to use Muan stock in their proposed civilization, but inculcated with the ancient Alantide ideology, which was ever a belief in rule of the many by the favored few. We of Mu believed always in communal cooperation."

York nodded.

"We will go to the surface and fight the Three Eternals," he said, glad to have an ally of such merit. "At present, they think we are dead and—"

York stopped short.

Vera gave a vocal cry, feeling the delicate mental probe of the Three in her femininely sensitive brain.

In a split second of time, before the probe had focused, she warned her husband and Kaligor to close their minds.

York commended her with his eyes, and they forced their minds in a telepathic short circuit.

Kaligor had caught on instantly, and likewise stood mentally inert.

Chapter 8

Vera heaved a sigh an hour later. The probe had gone.

"Lead the way," Kaligor said to York. "Up to the surface world, with your brain wave excavator."

It took them a month, York and Vera alternately forming the tunnel slanting upward. They became skilled in producing food, water, and air, when needed. Kaligor stalked after them silently, needing none of these necessities of life. Deathless he truly was.

As they neared the surface, he betrayed increasing excitement. To see the Sun again, the bustle of life, after twenty thousand years of caged dreams! At times, however, Kaligor seemed wrapped in a mental fog. The artificial vocal cords with which he was equipped murmured his ancient tongue. York and Vera caught the tailings of their mental origins—brief flashes of a strange, incredible Universe, peopled with non-existent beings!

Once the robot-bodied man stopped, confused, and it was an hour before York could convince him it was Earth, and not the dream stuff of Wolkia. Kaligor shook his head sadly.

"I live in two worlds," he murmured. "I will never be sure which is real! Too long, too long have I dwelt in that other land!"

Vera was invaluable as their sentinel against discovery by the Three Eternals' periodic, suspicious probings with their long-range mental detector, from their laboratory on Mount Olympus. Her quick mind detected instantly what the two blunter male minds might have noticed seconds too late. At her signals, they locked their minds instantaneously.

They emerged in Australia, as York had carefully planned, for it would have been disaster to burst through into the Pacific's watery bottom. York and Vera breathed free air thankfully, exulting in the warm sunlight that bathed their skins.

Kaligor leaned against a rock, his strangely flexible body trembling. Free at last of his horribly entombed fate, his was the emotion of a resurrected soul, mistakenly buried, a million times intensified.

Their thoughts expanding, free of the underground, they were not on guard.

"The mental probe!" Vera screamed suddenly.

They closed their minds—but a second too late. The mental gimlet became a battering force, trying to pry further. It was all they could do to resist. Kaligor waved silently and began running. After a mile, the force slipped away, off focus.

"Lost the range," panted York. "I don't think they found exactly where we are, in that short time. Only that we're somewhere in Australia. But now they do know we're alive! We must get to my space ship, in Sol City, as soon as possible. At least in that, if they find us, we can fly away."

Constantly on guard now, they set out. In a week they had crossed jungle and desert, reaching a busy seaport. Not disclosing their identity, passing themselves off as explorers and Kaligor as a mechanical robot little different from those in use for menial labors, they boarded a strato-liner for Sol City.

Lacking the necessary paper "money"—units of work based on a technological system—York employed hypnotism to delude the officials into believing he had paid for the passage.

But such details were trivial in dealing with the world of mortals. The burning thought before them was the coming battle to save civilization from the merciless hands of the Three Eternals.

Arriving in Sol City, they hastened to York's space ship, parked in a drome. Once inside, York drew his first easy breath in all those days. He sailed the ship out of the drome, up into the sky. Motioning Vera to the controls, he told her to set a course for the South Pacific, while he set down from memory the data of his subterranean exploration of geological stresses.

"The first thing to do is explode the key island that will counteract the rise of Atlantis and Mu," he said. "After that, we will reckon with the Eternals."

Kaligor nodded, his manner charged with anticipation of soon facing the Three who had thought to bury him for all eternity.

Vera was thoughtful. "I wonder why they haven't probed for us in the past few hours," she murmured quizzically. "Tony, it's ominous."

They knew the answer a few hours later, as they slanted down toward the tiny atoll that must be blasted. There, waiting for them, glinting in the sunlight, was a greenish-hulled ovoid ship.

"The Eternals!" gasped Vera.

York stopped his ship and snapped on his electro-protective screen, expecting immediate battle. But instead, the clear telepathic voice of the Three Eternals sounded.

"So, Anton York, you managed to escape your rockbound prison. We again deplore our underestimation of you. How did you do it?"

York was silent.

"No matter," came the unruffled tele-voice. "After detecting you with our mental probe, in Australia, and failing to pick you up again, we came here, knowing this would be your destination. We have one thing to thank you for—you have made things interesting for us, lightening our age-long ennui. If only you could oppose us further, give us a stirring fight, we would be grateful for the diversion!"

Mockery? Not exactly, it came to York. There was a core of sincerity behind the ironic words.

The Eternals went on. "But, of course, you cannot oppose us. Our twenty thousand years of science will crush your two thousand. We—" The psychic voice stiffened a little. "There is a third person, or mind, aboard your ship. Who—"

Kaligor's flexible body had been trembling at this time, listening to the words of his ancient, bitter enemies. Now he took an unnecessary step forward.

"It is I, Kaligor!" boomed out the Muan's tele-voice. "Do you remember me?"

"Kaligor!"

It was a startled chorus from all three Eternals. A moment later a queer ultralight flicked into the cabin, from the other ship. It moved about and finally centered on the robot. Like a detached eye, it roved up and down his body, and it seemed to express amazed bewilderment.

Finally the Eternals broke their shocked silence.

"Yes, it is you, Kaligor. Our tele-eye shows you on our screen. It cannot lie. You were freed by Anton York?"

Taking evident delight in the telling, Kaligor briefly recounted his rescue.

"Thus I face you again, Three Eternals, like a ghost from the past!" he challenged.

"Kaligor—with Anton York!" The involuntary thought of one of the Eternals, barely perceptible, was a betrayal, as though the combination struck fear. Then hastily: "But no matter. We are about to destroy your ship, and you, Anton York. Kaligor, though indestructible, you will fall to the bottom of the sea. We will capture you again, seal you at the center of Earth perhaps, where no one will blunder in to set you free. You will lie there, spinning your endless dream further, while up here we will snuff out this Mu-spawn civilization and build the second Atlantide era."

"You are senile, mentally if not physically," taunted Kaligor. "Atlantis, and all it stood for, are things of the past. Muan principles and culture will endure. I, Kaligor, say it and—"

At that moment, the Three Eternals opened fire. A soundless blast of energy sprang against York's electro-screen. The screen held, but succeeding blasts began to send a warning needle higher and higher toward the red danger mark of penetration. One touch of the disintegration beam on the hull and the ship would fall together like a rotten gourd.

York wasted no time firing back, remembering the last encounter where his gamma-sonic weapon had been so ineffective. He fled toward open space, before they brought their paralysis beam to bear.

"Fool!" he cursed himself. "I should have suspected they'd be waiting here. We should have thought of armament first."

Up the ship arrowed. In free space, York tried his best acceleration, but the green ship of the Eternals clung on the trail relentlessly and drew steadily closer. Any principle of super-velocity York had discovered in his two thousand years of research must be known to the Eternals. And more.

"Tony, what can we do?" Vera moaned.

"Kaligor!" York appealed, in turn. "Can you think of anything?"

There was no answer from the robot, slumped in a corner of the cabin.

"Kaligor!" yelled York frantically.

The Muan started, raised his faceless head.

"What? Is that you, Binti? No—no—what am I saying? Her name is Vera York! What is this world? Tell me. I'm confused."

"Earth, Kaligor!" groaned York. "Come out of your dream world. The Three Eternals—"

A flash of blinding light, as the enemy's gas-ray rammed into their screen, brought Kaligor to full awareness.

"The brain wave, York! Use that Command their screen to fall away!"

York tried it, wondering how he had stupidly failed to think of it himself. Vera took the controls. York stared fixedly out at the enemy ship, concentrating. He threw every ounce of his brain power into the mental command for the Eternals' protective screen to break down, then fired his gamma-sonic weapon.

But the telekinetic force that had molded hard stone like putty failed to crush the super-powerful screen of the Eternals. It was pure energy battling pure energy, again. The only noticeable effect was that the green ship fell back for an instant, as though it had struck something.

York tried again and again, his mind reeled with the draining effort. Each time the enemy ship faltered a little, but its screen held. Staggering, York slipped the brain wave concentrator out of his ear and handed it to Kaligor.

"You try it!" he gasped.

Kaligor held the tiny instrument before his forehead. York and Vera could not see on his featureless face the mental concentration he brought to bear, but the ship of the Eternals bounced back a minute later after each repeated blow of telekinetic force. "Their screen is adamant," said Kaligor. "They'll win out in the end, unless—"

Rapidly, he outlined a plan. York nodded and waited tensely.

Chapter 9

Kaligor once more faced the oncoming ship, through the port window. York and Vera could almost feel the tremendous mental forces he was concentrating, second by second. Kaligor released a blast of telekinetic force, a minute later, that hurled the green ship back and back until it vanished in the blackness of space.

At the same time, as they had planned, York shot their ship sideward at a prodigious pace. Then, in successive arcs, he warped their course at a random angle to the last position.

"Enough!" barked Kaligor, five minutes later. "Shut off the motor, the screen, every generator—and close your minds!" Obeying, the three now drifted in a silent, dark ship as inert as any meteor in space. They felt the mental probe of the Eternals, trying to locate them, but an hour later it ceased. A broadcast telepathic voice rolled over them.

"You have escaped for the time being, Kaligor and Anton York," admitted the Eternals. "But we have won. We will go back to Earth, and set up a headquarters on the very island you would have to destroy, to save the Muan civilization. We will wait, on guard. If you return, we will destroy you. When the ancient lands have arisen, and we have constructed Atlantide civilization, we will search you out, in whatever remote corner of the Universe—for the final reckoning!"

Vera signaled the two men to keep their minds locked, when they were about to relax. Understanding, for it might be a ruse to discover them, they waited. It was not till three hours later that they cautiously opened their minds. No mental probe greeted them.

"They've gone back to Earth," sighed York, "as they said." He went on heavily. "They have won. We know now that we can't penetrate their screen. They can ours, in a longer battle."

"But, Tony, why can't we build a better screen, and find some force to penetrate theirs?" suggested Vera.

York shook his head. "It would take years—centuries! In that time, civilization will be destroyed, the very thing we're trying to save. Don't you see, Vera? The Eternals are eighteen thousand years ahead of us. Ahead of Kaligor, too, for he lay impotent, dreaming, for that long time while they crawled up on the scale of science."

"Impotent! Dreaming!" Kaligor gave a mental sigh. "Yes, dreaming. Ah, if I could only use some of the science of my dream world! Mirbel and Binti, that time they fought the triple minds of Kashtal, had a wonderful weapon… But it is no use. Their science was of the six-dimensional Universe, useless in ours. All dream stuff, all, all—"

York and Vera almost pitied him, as he faded away into his dream world again, where all harsh realities could be solved.

"There's only one hope," pondered York. "Developing the telekinetic force. If we made a larger concentrator, one for all three of our minds at once, we might get a large enough blast out of it to smash their screen, instead of just pushing them away. What do you think of that, Kaligor?"

But Kaligor was lost in his dream, and Vera firmly silenced York's half angry shouts to awake him.

"Tony," she said softly, "waking from a beautiful dream is the worst feeling in all the world. Let poor Kaligor break into waking life gradually. He has been twenty thousand years in that other world—only a few days in ours!"

A week later, after a slow, careful cruise lest the Eternals detect them with long-range finders, they landed on an isolated section of the Moon, away from mining outposts.

Despite their grim situation, it amused them to tune into the radio news from the world of mortals.

"A dozen more ships have now docked, with burned-out instruments, and reported the same mysterious occurrence of last week, out in space somewhere between Earth and Moon," said one announcer. "Without warning, loose energy of some sort surged in that area, burning out all radios, lighting systems, and intership phones. Dr. Emanuel Harper, famous physicist, estimates that some forty-five trillion ergs of energy were expended in a few minutes, at some point thousands of miles away from his particular ship.

"This would be enough energy to light all of Sol City for three thousand years! It was all scattered away in a few minutes. Who or what could do that? Is Anton York out there somewhere? What is he doing? A thousand years ago he moved planets. Is he preparing some similar engineering feat, to again astound mankind?"

Vera smiled wanly. "Another chapter in the mythology of Anton York is writing itself. The truth they would not even believe!"

Pooling their scientific knowledge, Kaligor and York, worked out a large-sized brain wave concentrator. In the workshop room of York's ship was every conceivable scientific tool. For raw material they used the molecules of the Lunar terrain, shaping them into any metal or product with applied chemical telekinesis.

They tested the machine one day. All three of them poured a combined mental command into the receiver. With creaks and groans that they felt as vibration through the ship, a nearby Lunar mountain moved back ten feet!

"Remember that old Biblical adage, Vera?" said York, awed himself. "'If ye have faith, ye can move a mountain!'" York had moved much greater things at one time—whole worlds in fact. But he had used world-moving energies produced through gigantic machines. What they had done now had been done purely through mind, with the veriest of thoughts. And thoughts were limitless in scope.

They could have commanded the mountain to dance away and plunge into space at the speed of light, had they wished. Even so, would this great new force prevail against the ultra-scientific Eternal Three?

They sailed to Earth, boldly now. The Three Eternals had already begun construction of a marble home, like that on Mount Olympus, on the key island in the Pacific. Their green-hulled ship came to meet them. Over the ocean waters they battled.

The Eternals hurled their Jovian charges of energy against York's screen, rapidly wearing it down. Keeping their nerves in check, York, Vera and Kaligor stood before their brain wave projector. At Kaligor's signal, they thrust a common mental command into the receiver.

A measurelessly powerful telekinetic beam leaped for the enemy ship. But nothing happened. Its screen did not buckle, as they had hoped.

And the ship itself did not even budge one inch, where at least it should have been dashed away!

"Failed, didn't it?" came the taunting telepathic voice from the Three Eternals. "We managed to deduce it was telekinetic force with which you escaped last time. We've installed a simple enough counter radiator that split your beam and caused it to flow around your ship."

Beyond, where the split beam rejoined and angled down to the ocean's broad bosom, water churned madly. A mile-wide hole appeared, clapped together again and sent a mile-high wall of water rolling toward distant shores. Hours later, several coastal cities of mortal man would be wrecked by the greatest "tidal wave" in history.

"And now," came the frosty announcement, "prepare for death!"

A particularly vicious blast shook York's ship and nearly burst through his screen. York jerked his ship up and away. Flight again! But with no hope this time of escape.

So it seemed. Hounding them, the Eternals' ship prepared to send its final barrage against York's tattered screen, in another moment—annihilation.

But queerly, the Eternals suddenly lost the range. Their ship blundered past, almost striking them, and went on, as though searching. Soon it had lost itself in the curtain of space. York saw then that Kaligor was still standing before the telekinesis projector.

Only now he turned away.

"Hypnosis," he explained wearily, as though it had drained all his mind. "I hypnotized them into the belief that we had suddenly become invisible. Change course quickly, York. They will be back in an instant. It won't work twice."

York, as once before, shifted the ship at random arcs till they were far from their original position. The Eternals did not appear. Safe, for the time being.

They hardly spoke to one another in the next hour, as their ship cruised slowly in space. With the brain wave projector useless against the Eternals, they could think of no other weapon or force to try.

"But we have to do something," said York haggardly. "We can't give up. Kaligor, is there anything—anything—" Kaligor shrugged wearily and lapsed into his escape world of dreams. York almost envied him and wished that he might dream so pleasantly. But York's dreams, lately, had been nightmares in which the Three Eternals endlessly chased him to the remotest corners of space and time.

Vera smiled at him wanly.

"You must rest, Tony," she admonished gently. "Let's forget about the Three Eternals for awhile. Maybe our minds, fresher, will think of something later. Let's look out at the peaceful stars."

They turned out the cabin lights and sat arm in arm before a wide port, gazing out at the star-powdered vault of the firmament. They talked over their many wanderings in space, trying to forget the maddening menace behind them. Venus gleamed brilliantly among the stars.

"Remember bringing an asteroid to Venus, as its new moon?" murmured Vera. "How happy we were in that accomplishment. So many Earth settlers sighed for moonlight, through the long Venusian nights."

She felt her husband start slightly.

"Vera!" he whispered tensely. "You've given me an idea. Suppose we towed away another asteroid, took it to Earth. Suppose we gave it a tremendous velocity, and aimed it for the key island. Even the Eternals wouldn't be able to stop trillions of tons of hard rock plunging down without warning upon their heads!"

York woke Kaligor, after much mental shouting, and outlined the plan to him. "Good!" agreed the Muan.

Once more hope went with them as they maneuvered far from Earth's vicinity, out to the barren asteroids. After some search, they singled out a dense little body roughly five miles in diameter. Their ship was no more than a grain of sand beside it, but before long they were nudging it out of its age-old orbit, with the illimitable forces of their telekinetic projector.

Hour by hour it gained velocity, in the long stretch of space toward Earth.

York spent brain-numbing hours over the equations of its course. He had to hit precisely one certain spot on Earth, the while it inexorably continued to revolve and rotate. It took timing to seven decimal places. It was super-ballistics, with the asteroid in the role of a gigantic shell shot from a mythical cannon against a target that moved in the four dimensions of space time.

"And yet," he summed it up, when done, "it's really easier to figure this hundred-million-mile trajectory in space than it would be to aim a cannon shot on Earth for a mere thousand miles. The motions and laws of space are precise, unvarying. Those on Earth are subject to the vagaries of wind, temperature and air density. I think we'll be able to land the asteroid squarely on the island, at a speed of a hundred miles a second."

It took them two weeks to push the asteroid within striking distance. Gradually its velocity had mounted. It had been aimed unerringly to reach Earth's orbit, plunge into its atmosphere, and drop like a great bomb on the island of the Three Eternals.

"It can't fail!" said Kaligor confidently, rechecking York's figures for the third time. "The Eternals will have no warning. The asteroid is too small to shine as a moving star except in the last few minutes. It will light incandescently when it strikes the atmosphere, but a few seconds later it will land. The Eternals will be ground flat into the Earth itself! And at the same time, the island will be cracked apart, reversing the rise of Atlantis. York, it is a splendid plan!"

"I hope it works."

Now that the zero moment approached, York was assailed by doubts. Yet how could the Eternals survive it, this hurling of a world at them?

Chapter 10

Reaching a point a thousand miles above Earth, York halted his ship. The asteroid plunged on. It vanished from their sight. Then, five seconds later it reappeared, glowing slightly. With each passing second, as it hurtled into the thicknesses of the atmosphere, it brightened.

Like a glowing diamond, it plummeted for the ground—and the island. It had been aimed perfectly.

"Here's a little present for you, Eternals!" sang out Kaligor, moving for the ship's telescope.

It struck!

Watching, they saw it shatter into a shower of sparks, from their perspective, that spattered far over the Pacific Ocean. Dense clouds of steam shot skyward. More than a quadrillion tons of rock had smashed into Earth, the impact was sufficient to affect, by a measurable split second, the rotation of the planet. Earthly astronomers would later notice that, and record the fall of the largest meteorite in history, little suspecting the man-made agency behind it.

York drew a deep breath. That mighty mass had rocketed straight down upon the marble home of the Three Eternals. By no stretch of imagination could they have survived.

"York!"

Kaligor, at the telescope, had given the sharp mental cry.

"The marble building is still intact! The asteroid struck some shell of force over it, broke on that, and the pieces simply slid off into the ocean on all sides!"

He followed this stunning, incredible announcement with an urgent warning.

"Quickly! Lights off, ship unpowered, minds closed! They will be after us in a moment. We're safer here than in trying to outdistance them after detection."

They waited for long hours, minds locked against mental probing, realizing the Eternals would not dare leave their island unless they detected the position of their quarry.

At last, as before, a broadcast telepathic message rustled in their minds.

"Did you think to catch us unawares, Kaligor and Anton York?" scoffed one of the Eternal Three. "We remembered that you had learned to move worlds before, Anton York. We expected you to try this. A trigger-touch dome of force protected the island and our home. Even if you should hurl the Moon down on us, we would shunt it aside. We dealt with world-moving forces long before you! Must we repeat over and over that you are as children to us? Children who must eventually be caught and punished?"

York went to his controls and eased the ship away from Earth, following a regular liner route so that the eternals' detectors would not single them out.

"Now what's left, Kaligor?" he asked, biting his lip. "What's left to try—and it'll be the last try!"

But Kaligor was sunk in the myths of his mind, in temporary escape from the stark, pressing problem that brought haggard lines to the faces of his two companions.

"Mirbel!" his mind was murmuring, as they had first heard it murmuring from inside the steel block. "Mirbel, is that you? And Binti! I have been to a strange dream world, called—let me think—Earth! Earth, yes. I dreamed of struggle, futile opposition to super-scientists. But that is impossible, isn't it, Mirbel? I'm the supreme scientist in the Universe! Binti, tell me it was a dream!"

Losing patience at last, York prodded the bemused Muan.

"Wake up, Kaligor! This is no time to dream. In the name of the Universe, stop mumbling and talking to those two. They're phantoms, figments, myths, dummies—do you understand?"

York was immediately sorry for his outburst. But Kaligor came awake.

"Phantoms! Figments!" he echoed. "Myths, dummies! Yes, you're right."

Suddenly his telepathic contact broke, became a rush of jumbled thought. For a moment York thought he had again dropped into his enchanted spell, but his telepathic voice resumed, now clear, strong.

"Anton York," he said, "what is most important in all this—ourselves or the civilization we are trying to save?"

"Civilization!" returned York without hesitation. "They are our people—yours and mine. They advance, slowly but surely." Firmly he repeated: "The civilization—for what it is to become. It must be preserved, even at the cost of our lives!"

York felt a strange embarrassment, with the last word, as though he had thrown it before the robot's face.

"I cannot die," said Kaligor evenly. "No, but I can sacrifice to an equal extent."

"What are you driving at?" York demanded.

"There is only one way to achieve that aim for which we would both make the final sacrifice," continued Kaligor. "By decoying the Three Eternals away from the island long enough to blow it up!"

Kaligor went on, and suddenly it was all starkly clear to York....

A year went by, a year in which York, Vera and Kaligor labored over intricate mechanisms.

Then, one day, they faced the Eternals once again at their island. Kaligor sat hunched at the controls of the ship. His telepathic radiation issued from a human brain, clothed in an unhuman shell. Their fleshly bodies offering sharp contrast York and Vera stood back of him, almost woodenly tense, as their plan was started.

"We have a new weapon," boasted Kaligor to the enemy. "One that will not fail, Eternals. Death comes to you—"

Kaligor jerked a lever and a queer reddish beam sprang toward the enemy ship. It spangled against their screen, spread like red paint, but nothing else happened.

"A puny force, no better than your others!" chorused the Eternals triumphantly. "Now you, Kaligor and Anton York, will greet that most final master—Death!"

Again York's screen blazed to near extinction, as the Eternals threw their heaviest beams against it. And York's ship fled for the fourth time, as though this were some play that must be enacted over and over again for all eternity.

Inside the ship, Kaligor manipulated the controls with his flexible, tentacular fingers. He drove the ship away at its utmost acceleration, arrowing into the open void. The more tender forms of York and Vera flattened against one wall, their eyes closing. Kaligor glanced at them and nodded in satisfaction. It would take the Eternals some time to catch up, at this super-pace.

On and on the chase went, at rates unknown and impossible to ordinary space ships that mankind knew. Mars flashed by, then the asteroids, Jupiter, and finally Pluto, and the two ships catapulted out into the outer immensity, exceeding the speed of light. This was the final pursuit. It could end in only one way.

* * * *

Kaligor felt the mental probe of the Three Eternals, playing over the unconscious forms of York and Vera, as though wondering what had happened to them. Even, for a moment, their visual teleray flicked about. Both probes left finally, and the chase went on. Kaligor, though he could not grin physically, was certainly grinning within his human mind.

Inevitably, the green-hulled ship crawled closer, closer. Finally, within range, it began to batter at the screen again. Kaligor watched the needle spin to the danger mark—and pass it. The screen was down!

Flame leaped into the ship, searing, scorching. Metal glowed and melted. The two mortal bodies of York and Vera, still unmoving, unconscious, were touched by naked fire and then they began to dance and writhe. But only for a moment. Soon they were gone, consumed.

"The final sacrifice!" murmured Kaligor, watching the ship burn away around him.

Everything was consumed around Kaligor. But his body could not be consumed. He was out in space, free, the ship and all it had contained disintegrated to the last atom. A multitude of fiery stars decorated all space, watching indifferently this battle between super-beings.

"Thus you have finally been defeated, Kaligor!" came the telepathic voice from the victorious Three Eternals. "Anton York and his mate are no more and you—you will float through space, at your present velocity, for all eternity! It is a better end for you than what we had planned!"

But no answer came from Kaligor, to his ancient enemies. Instead, they barely detected a faint rumble.

"Binti! Mirbel! How good to see you again! I have just awakened from that dream. That dream of—what is it?—Earth! Binti, Mirbel, you are real. Not those others. They called you phantoms, Mirbel, and you, sweet Binti. They said you were just myths, figments of a dream I had spun in a long sleep. What was that other word? Yes, dummies. They called you dummies, and somehow, in that other dream of Earth, it was very significant, that word. Very significant, but I can't remember—I can't remember... Binti... Mirbel... I will stay with you now—"

"Dummies!"

One of the Three Eternals roared that to the others. "Did you hear? I see it all now. We've been decoyed, lured away, while back on Earth—"

York, back on Earth, turned away from the mind concentrator with which he had been projecting his thoughts out into space. Impinging on a delicate relay within the cleverly wrought dummy of himself aboard Kaligor's ship, his mind had been there—as far as the Three Eternals' mental probe had determined. Vera's too. Now there was no reaction from the dummy-relay, proving the Eternals had finally caught up with Kaligor, after a long three-hour chase.

"It worked, Vera!" York cried. "The Eternals have been decoyed at least beyond Pluto, thinking all the time that you and I were with Kaligor, when they were only life-like dummies. Organic robots, really, since they held our thoughts. And pretty cleverly made—artificial protoplasm, exact duplicates of us, in case the Eternals used a visual check-up. Most important of all, the mental-relays within the dummies' skull-cases."

He laughed almost gaily. "The Three Eternals were fooled by one of the simplest, oldest tricks in the Universe!"

Vera was less jubilant, more solemn. "Kaligor thought of it," she murmured. "His dream world was of some use after all. And now just think, Tony"—her voice became soft, pitying—"he must float on and on, in boundless space, never to know death. His sacrifice has been more, much more, than ours will be! And yet, perhaps, he would have it so. He will continue creating his mental universe, which he loves, and in which he—belongs. He will live in it! Perhaps—who really knows?—it is as real as ours, to us. Life is all in the mind—" Her voice trailed away moodily.

York nodded, subdued. Then he stirred himself and piloted his ship up and out of the dense island jungle in which it was hidden. It was his own ship. The one Kaligor had piloted away had been an outward duplicate, built secretly in Sol City's great factories.

"We have about three hours," said York, "before the Eternals come back. Three hours for which Kaligor traded an eternity of helpless drifting."

A few minutes later their ship hovered over the atoll marked for demolition, so that a geological process started years before might be reversed. York set his gamma-sonic weapon for instantaneous decomposition of the entire island to a depth of five miles. His generators were loaded to the full.

His lips pursed in anticipation as he depressed the button. Once again his unobtrusive violet ray shot forth from its gravity-fed power coils. Hissingly it struck the island, and the marble home of the absent Three Eternals, boring down at the speed of light.

Layers of matter peeled away and vanished in puffs of soot. Before the ocean waters roared in to fill the breech, the five-mile pit had been formed.

York flung his ship up at full speed as a spume of water spurted from the impact of walls of water crashing together with the force of solid steel. Down below, in the invisible depths of Earth that they had so recently quitted, a Titanic ground vibration had spawned. Like a match it would touch off the gunpowder of subsea plasma. There would be a clashing of Gargantuan forces, one started years before by the Eternals. For awhile the Behemoth of an earthquake would reign widely, on Earth's surface. But then it would be over, and Earth would be quiet…

Three hours later, York found confirmation of his success. The bubbles arising from the Pacific floor had lessened by half. Mu was halting its slow upward climb. And in the Atlantic, a continent buried for twenty thousand years in its watery grave also ceased to seek an unnatural resurrection.

"It is done!" breathed York, with quiet pride.

Vera's face strained for the past days, grew yet more haggard.

"It is done!" she repeated, but with a deeper meaning. Suddenly she was in his arms, sobbing. "Is there no escape, Tony?"

"I'm afraid not," returned York, gently. "The Three Eternals will seek their vengeance. They are powerful beyond measure, as we know. It would do little good to try to hide, in space. Their long-range instruments would search us out, even light years away. Kaligor made his sacrifice. We must make ours, as we agreed." He raised his head. "But Earth is saved. Earth gave us life. Kaligor too. We must think of it that way, my darling of the ages!"

Vera dashed the tears from her eyes, bravely.

"We have lived, a full life, Tony dearest. Love, understanding, and wisdom beyond the lot of ordinary humans have been ours. We have touched the stars for a brief moment, reveled for a bit of eternity. Dreamed a beautiful dream of immortality, like Kaligor. But we could not escape the laws of Fate, as we did the laws of life. It is over and I am content!"

They kissed, and clung to one another tightly, in their last embrace. Like gods they had lived, but unlike gods, they must die. The finger of a greater destiny had so decreed.

Not long after, the powerful telepathic voice of the Three Eternals beat in upon their minds. Their ship appeared, dropping from the sky vulturously. Bluntly, seeing the key-island destroyed, they promised swift death. York spun his ship away, as though trying to escape the inevitable. The large ovoid ship of the Three followed inexorably.

Pursued and pursuing, they shot far into space, out among the emptiness they both knew so well. When they had gone so far that York knew Earth could not be harmed by what was to come, he stopped. Grimly, he set his giant gravity coils, loaded to capacity with world-moving power. Then he smiled as he took Vera in his arms to await the end calmly.

Unknowing of his voluntary sacrifice, the Three Eternals rammed toward his ship enough power to grind it to subatomic shreds. It was like the lighting of a bomb. York's ship released its groaning load of energy in one colossal charge. The ether itself writhed.

Both ships vanished! Back on Earth, every electrical instrument burned out entirely from the mighty reaction waves that had resulted.

They were gone, the gods that Earth knew. Greek mythology and the mythology of Anton York would carry on the legends of their exploits, in distorted form. But the gods themselves were one with infinity. But there would be no mythology of Kaligor, the Eternal Dreamer. Indestructible, falling perhaps eventually into the hot core of some sun, his dream would go on...on...

THE SECRET OF ANTON YORK

PROLOGUE

At the top of Mount Everest stand two gigantic statues of enduring diamond, a hundred feet tall. Gleaming in the stratosphere, they rear higher than any other man-made object on Earth's surface, as the two after whom they had been modeled rear higher than any others in human history.

Those were the statues modeled after the immortal Anton York and his mate.

In the year of their commemoration, 4050 A.D., the President of the Solar System Council spoke to a gathered crowd of ten million, and to a television audience of ten billion on nine planets. His voice was emotion-filled and awed, as though he spoke of gods.

"Anton York and his wife are dead. But Anton York's name will live, alongside those of Alexander, Caesar, Napoleon and other empire builders. And Confucius, Christ, Mohammed and other spiritual leaders. And Adam, Jove, Robin Hood and other mythological names. For Anton York was like all these in one respect or more.

"He was born in the twentieth century. Preserved by his father's life-elixir, he lived on, immortally. These great exploits will ring down the hall of history: His defeat of the fifty Immortals who wished to subjugate Earth, in the twenty-first century. His legacy of space-travel to mankind, soon after. His defeat of Mason Chard, the last of the ruthless Immortals, in the thirty-first century. His astro-engineering in the Solar System, giving Jupiter rings, moons to Mercury and Venus, and ridding all the planets of harsh obstacles to colonization.

"But the greatest of all was his return from the deeps of space, in our present time, to wage some titanic battle against the mysterious Three Eternals, who wished to destroy contemporary civilization. We do not even know the true story of it, save in snatches. We know only that the Three Eternals, survivors from some forgotten time—perhaps Atlantis—pursued Anton York's space ship out beyond Pluto, a year ago.

"An astronomer's plates, on that dark outpost, caught something of the event. The space ship of the Three Eternals hurled some destructive force at York's ship. The latter seemed loaded with mighty energies. Both ships vanished in an explosion that must have rocked the Universe from one end to another. Pluto was shoved a million miles out of its orbit by etheric concussion!"

He paused to let the worlds imagine the incredible fury of that scene.

"We can only surmise at what mighty, unknown forces were released. And we can only wonder why York, to destroy the Three Eternals, sacrificed himself. Evidently he could defeat the Eternals only in that way, in a battle of gods.

"Of one thing we are sure. The incredible career of Anton York is over. We are gathered here to commemorate his memory, in the most lasting material we know, on this highest peak of Earth's entire surface."

The speaker looked over the solemn, hushed multitude packed at the base of the towering mountain. He delivered his funereal text.

"Anton York, benefactor of humanity, is dead!"

Chapter 1

Those words, if they could have rolled by some magic throughout the greater cosmos, would eventually have impinged on the ears of the person in question, and made him smile.

For Anton York was alive.

Yet he had not been sure of that himself, at first. With a shock his brain had awakened. His staring eyes focused on the cabin wall of his ship. It looked as it had always been. But queerly, he saw two walls. It was a doubling effect, as if two superimposed images lay on one another. And he could not move. He was in the grip of some paralysis that locked every muscle in his body, including his lungs and heart. He was not breathing and his blood, chilled and viscous, lay stagnant in his veins.

Yet he was alive, for his thoughts were free. Or was this death?

His thoughts probed out in mental telepathy, which he had used so often with his wife. He could not turn to look.

"Vera!" his mind called. "Vera, are you near?"

Her mental voice came back, confused, dim.

"Yes, Tony. I hear you. You must be near. I feel as though we are mental wraiths. Is this the life-after-death? How wonderful, Tony, not to be separated after all—" Her psychic tone became startled. "But look! This is the cabin of our ship, even if it appears double somehow. It was destroyed in that frightful explosion caused by the Three Eternals. How can a material ship pass into the life-after-death?"

It was a grimly ridiculous thought.

"No, Vera." York's thoughts were reflective. "The ship wasn't destroyed. Nor were we. It's sheer speculation, but perhaps the explosion acted so suddenly and so powerfully that it blew the ship away intact. Like tornado winds that blow straws right through oak boards without knocking off one grain. Vera, we're alive!"

"But this paralysis—"

"Suspension of life, through the shock of super-fast motion. Germs, in centrifuges whirled at high speed, pass into a dormant state, as Earth scientists know. All our cells have gone as a unit into suspended animation."

"You mean that we'll stay helpless like this? For ages, thinking, thinking..." Vera's psychic voice was alarmed, half hysterical.

"No," York answered quickly. "Don't forget we have twice the normal number of life-giving radiogens in our cells. Cosmic rays are constantly pouring into them. The energy stored will sooner or later break the deadlock. We just have to wait."

Cosmic radiation fed itself into their immortality radiogens. Electrical energy, the warmth of life in the last analysis, gradually built up as in a storage battery. The stunned cells, knocked out by the force of the super-explosion, slowly returned to normal.

It took a year.

During that time, happy at escaping the death that had seemed inexorable, they conversed mentally. They spoke of things past, wondering of things present, and looked forward to things future, once they were free. Well inured to the dragging of time in their 2,000 years of life, the short year passed quickly to them, where it might have driven an ordinary mortal mad.

Anton York felt the twitch of some buried muscle one day. Others came alive quickly, as if it were a signal. The involuntary muscles instantly took up their given tasks. The heart beat and the diaphragm pumped up and down, sucking air into the lungs.

York leaped up suddenly, only to collapse again with a groan. The atrophied muscles refused to take up their burden that quickly.

A few minutes later he arose again, stronger, and turned to help Vera up. He supported her while her body went through the same phases. Finally they embraced each other, knowing the supreme joy of life, when death had seemed inevitable.

"Tony, dearest, are we truly immortal?" Vera spoke, using her vocal chords instead of the tiring telepathy. They noticed immediately that the sound echoed, in the same queer doubling effect of their vision. She went on. "Disease and old age can't touch us. Now even that terrible explosion, violent death, failed! We're like the legendary gods."

"Don't think that way!" York returned almost sharply. "We must never lose our perspective. We're immortals through science. And some principle of science accounts for our escape. I had our energy coils loaded to capacity with power enough to shatter a sun. When the Three Eternals shoved a dis-beam at us and released it, the explosion acted on every atom simultaneously, blowing ship and all away as a unit. Probably at the speed of light and out into remote space."

"The Three Eternals!" Vera burst in suddenly. "If they survived the explosion too, they may be near now, ready to blast us again—"

York, reminded of their deadly enemies, was already leaping toward the visiscreen, for an all-around view of surrounding space. Like their eyes, the view-plate seemed afflicted with the singular doubling effect. The firmament of stars around them contained all pairs. But no alien ship blocked out any part of the sky.

"The Eternals aren't here," York announced, his nerves easing. "They must have been destroyed then—no, wait! I see their ship now. Just a speck far away, where they were blown in a different direction."

Vera bent close to the view-plate suddenly.

"And look. Another ship is approaching theirs! A queer ship—"

"Hsst!" York warned. A totally alien ship might be friend or enemy. "Tune in mentally, if you make contact with the Three Eternals."

Opening their minds full range, they waited to hear any telepathic radiations from the distant scene. At last they heard a voice, in the universal language of telepathy. Yet they recognized it for an alien, non-human voice, by its mental overtones.

"What ship is this?" challenged the voice, as though it were a patrol ship on the high seas. "Answer immediately!"

York and Vera waited breathlessly. At last one of the Three Eternals answered groggily, as though he, too, had just emerged from the same suspended state following the explosion.

"The ship of the Three Eternals. We just survived a tremendous explosion, miraculously."

"Who are you? Where are you from?" The psychic voice was staccato, peremptory.

"From Earth." And then, typically, the Eternal spoke angrily. "But who are you to make demands? I resent your insolence."

"Earth!" It seemed to be a startled exclamation from the alien. "The J-X seventy-seven creatures! You've come to rescue—" The words broke off. Then came a horribly merciless tone. "I am sorry."

In the view-plate, York and Vera saw a green energy-ray stab from the alien ship to the Three Eternals. In a supernal flash of sparks, the ship of the Three Eternals vanished!

The black dot of the alien ship hovered for a moment, as though to make sure of their work. Then it scudded away, disappearing into the void beyond.

Vera shuddered. "I'm glad the Three Eternals are gone, though I've never wanted the death of a human before. They were such evil beings."

"Evil beings?" York's voice was tense. "What about those ruthless aliens? They did us a favor, destroying the Three Eternals, but we'd get the same if they found us. Who are they? From what system? Why are they patrolling space?"

Vera had no answer.

"I wonder where we are," York mused. "We have a lot of things to do and find out. First, this queer doubling of our sight and voices."

A strange expression came over his face. He strode to his laboratory workroom and for the next few hours labored with his intricate instruments. Vera brought in hot food, in answer to their reawakened appetites. She found her husband tapping his finger on the barrel of an electronic spectorscope. He was frowning, and behind the frown was startled disbelief.

"Tony," Vera asked, "have you found out where we are? Let's return to Earth. I don't like the thought of meeting those aliens."

"Return to Earth?" York had started. He gripped her shoulders. "I just made a rough measurement of the velocity of light here. It's only a hundred-and-eighty-one miles a second—five thousand miles a second slower than it should be! And the velocity of sound is quite a bit below eleven hundred feet per second!"

"That accounts for the doubling phenomenon," Vera returned quickly, for she was no less of a scientist than her husband. "Our eyes and ears are attuned to different rates. But, Tony, you look so worried." At the same instant it struck her. "Why should light and sound travel slower?" she gasped.

For an answer, York swept his hand toward the nearest port. Out there lay the eternal stars, but what had happened to them? Even they were changed. In their many lifetimes of wandering, Anton York and Vera had come to know the star map almost as minutely as one knows the streets of a city.

"Those are not our stars," York said in a low voice. "Vera, this is not the Universe we used to know!"

After eating in stunned silence, York spoke again, more calmly.

"I see it quite clearly now. The explosion blew us up as a unit—completely out of normal space-time—into a new universe! I've suspected for some time that different universes lie side by side, or wrapped up in one another. They occupy the same space and time, but not the same space-time. Notice that distinction. It's like taking two chemical reagents and mixing them in various proportions, to get many different compounds.

"This space-time, with its 'shorter' time and 'longer' space—judging from the low light speed—is separate and distinct from our Universe. Yet the two universes are contained in one another like alcohol in water. Earth, in one sense, is no more than a few miles away in space and a few hours in time. In another sense, it's remoter than the most distant nebula and several eternities removed on an all-embracing time scale."

Vera's brows came together over a white anxious face.

"Tony, it confuses me. I'm afraid. I feel as if we're dropping into an endless pit here. I never felt that way in our space. Tony, let's go back to our Universe right away."

He shook his head, telling her with his eyes to prepare for a greater shock.

"We can't At least for the present. Our engine, our energy-coils, our generators—all our motivating machines are dead. I tried them. You see, there's slower energy here too. We're marooned in this other universe, and drifting like a wandering comet. We're helpless, too. If those patrolling aliens happen to spy us…"

York left the rest ominously unsaid.

Chapter 2

But this did not happen. In the following year, York spent mind-numbing hours in his laboratory. Vera took down an endless series of notes. Together they sought to readjust their science to the new conditions.

In one thing, nature's laws of compensation were automatic. Their eyes and ears learned gradually to work under new conditions. The irksome doubling effects disappeared. But all else was still a mystery.

York became irritable.

"I'm getting nowhere," he raged. "I feel as helpless as a baby. In our Universe I had a wealth of super-science, by Earthly standards, at my fingertips. Now I can't even make a single reaction motor. Rockets here don't obey Newton's Third Law! It's getting me down. I'm like a Stone Age man looking around and wondering what it's all about. And, Vera, I don't like it."

He went on, betraying a nervousness he had kept under control rigidly.

"The Three Eternals had no chance to fight back when they were destroyed. Neither would we, if that patrol ship found us. But that isn't all."

Both knew without saying that there were other dangers. Already their stored air and food supplies were running low. In their own Universe, York would have laughed and transmuted oxygen and protein from sheer metal, bending the atoms to his will. But here, in a maddening universe with a new set of laws and measurements, he had less command over circumstances than a Neanderthal Man in some 20th century city.

"That sun, Tony," Vera whispered. "It's far past first magnitude now. We're drifting straight toward it. Another year—"

She left the appalling thought unfinished. In another year, unless they achieved a workable motor, they would fall into the huge, blazing sun. For a year it had grown steadily brighter athwart their drifting course. But they might starve first, or be caught by the patrol ship.

They had three ways to die, in this strange, mad universe, none of them pleasant.

The alien sun grew until it was the size of Sol from the distance of Pluto. They began to feel the slight acceleration, as its tentacles of gravity clutched at their ship. It was a strange, huge star, red as Antares.

Periodically, every twenty-two days, it increased in brightness. At its maximum it was almost blue-hot. Then it declined to the red state again. On and on the cycle went, with the precise regularity of a delicately made clock.

"A Cepheid variable," York said. "Like the Cepheids of our universe, it obeys some mysterious law of waxing and waning atomic-disintegration in its interior. And similarly, if the balance slips at some time, it will explode into a flaming nova. These are very unstable stars. If there are planets—"

He searched with his telescope. It was small, but through a principle of television magnification, had a resolving power ten times greater than a 200 inch reflector. He swept all the regions around the pulsing sun.

"Yes, it has planets, thirteen of them," he announced finally. "We're drifting toward the tenth outermost. We won't fall into the sun after all, Vera. We'll crash on that planet!"

He was grimly humorous.

"Radio." Vera clutched at straws. "An SOS signal might bring rescue."

"Or that patrol ship." York shook his head. "But I don't think their race is here at all. This Cepheid sun sheds an extremely variable radiation. Any planet here must have a range of temperature that shoots from frigidity to super-tropical heat every twenty-two days. Evolution must have balked at trying to adjust creatures to such rapid changes." He laughed gratingly. "And in the first place, I can't signal an SOS. There's a new radio principle here, too."

He faced around haggardly.

"Only one chance, Vera. If I can get one little rocket working, we can land safely on that planet."

While the world enlarged to a dull slate orb in the next month, York labored without sleep. He took drugs that would have killed a-normal man, and phosphate foods that went directly to his brain without feeding his body. He trusted his tremendous vitality and the cosmic-fed radiogens to keep him alive.

A week before the deadline, a tiny clue came to him—for the first time, the basic laws of the new universe dimly formed in his striving brain. Earth scientists, thousands upon thousands of them, had taken several centuries to piece out the natural laws of Earth's Universe. Alone, in two years, York began to note down the first fundamental rules in a totally new and strange universe where even light-waves slowed down.

"Newton's Third Law, the one applied to rockets, has a clause here! The higher the energy, the slower the reaction. It's almost backward. That means a slow-burning fuel will do the trick where an explosive one won't. Now I'm getting somewhere."

"Hurry, Tony!"

The planet loomed now like a giant blue moon.

Hastily York constructed a wide rocket tube at the stern. Loaded with slow-burning phosphorus, it belched forth clouds of smoky vapor. It would be useless as a rocket in Earth's Universe. But here it propelled the ship forward with amazing power.

York skillfully maneuvered the ship into a spiral course around the planet, barely in time to stop a stonelike plunge. It lowered screamingly into the atmosphere. The globular craft landed, just before consuming the last of their phosphorus supplies. York and Vera were thrown violently against the wall.

Vera crawled to her husband, weeping in mixed joy and fright.

"Tony, we're safe! The ship held. Tony!"

Groggily he opened his eyes, stilling her alarm that he might have been killed.

"Yes, made it," he mumbled. "New universe can't beat us. Now let me sleep awhile—"

He slept for three days. When he awoke, he devoured the enormous quantity of hot foods Vera had held ready. York relaxed with a sigh. Then he reverted to normal after an ordeal that might have shattered the mind and health of an Earthly mortal. He relaxed only for a moment. Then he was at his instruments, testing outside conditions.

"Air unbreathable, mainly hydrocarbons. Temperature minus one hundred twenty, but rising. The Cepheid sun is building up to its maximum."

They looked out over the alien world. It was flat, barren, blanketed with white, frozen gases. But these were dissipating slowly, swirling up into the atmosphere.

In a week's time all the white gas-snow was gone. The previously barren loam stirred with life. Weird, saw-edged plant life burst forth and grew amazingly, at a visible rate. As the Cepheid luminary rose to its maximum, it poured down a flood of hot blue rays. Almost abruptly the environment became tropical. Pseudo-palms and ferns reached for the sky.

"Life, after all," marveled York. "But probably only plant forms, enjoying a brief 'summer' of less than two weeks before the Cepheid's decline to 'winter' radiation."

He made a sudden exclamation.

"No. I'm wrong again. See those scuttling little forms among the grasses, like rabbits and weasels? Animal life! Nature is more persistent than I thought. Well anyway, I'm almost sure rational beings could not have arisen."

"I think you're wrong again, Tony." Vera smiled. "Look there, just over the horizon. I saw it before you awoke. In the telescope it looks like the top of a transparent dome. It may be a city." She gasped suddenly, in remembrance. "Tony, suppose it's the city of the patrol ship!"

York started, but spoke calmly.

"Suppose it isn't. I'll take a look at that dome. I've been trying for ten days to adjust our gravity engine, without result. If there are intelligent beings, and if they're friendly, I can get the data from them. Or at least a few pointers about this crazy universe's laws."

Vera looked worried when he turned to leave.

"You're unarmed, Tony, and on a strange world. Please be careful."

"I won't take any chances," he promised. "We'll keep in telepathic rapport all the time I'm away."

Clad in his spacesuit, equipped with oxygen and temperature control, Anton York moved off into what had become a semi-jungle. As he suspected, the life around him was unstable. The trees were so pulpy that they fell apart at a push. A little spidery-legged creature with feathers ran against his boot. The soft blow killed it. Its body withered away on the spot. In its place, transparent grass shot up six inches in a minute and then crumbled in a gust of wind.

Swift life and swift decay was the rule here.

York plodded on. He felt like some wanderer in a ghost forest, or a jungle-man treading primeval wastes. All the science, weapons, command of natural forces that he had wielded in his own universe were nothing here. He was unarmed, helpless. In direct ratio to his distance from the ship, he grew more worried. What if that dome actually did hold the ruthless aliens who had annihilated the Three Eternals without a second's hesitation?

For the first time in 2,000 years, York felt insecure. Before, visiting hundreds of worlds, he had felt himself at least the equal of any other beings.

He resolved to use extreme caution when he reached the dome.

"That's right, Tony," came Vera's clear telepathic voice. She had read his thoughts. "At the slightest sign of danger, race back."

York came upon the dome suddenly. It was fringed about by rampant life blooming under the maximum rays of the Cepheid sun. He gasped. Of clear transparent material, its arc of curvature indicated that it must be at least ten miles in diameter and a thousand feet high at the peak. Only intelligence could have built the structure—first-class intelligence!

A second shock came when he looked in. He had expected a city, a mass of buildings, dwellings, busy crowds performing their daily tasks, bustling civilization, protected under the dome from the constantly changing environment outside. Such should be the logical explanation for this mighty, arcing shell.

But instead—

The scene inside was that of another world. Not a city, it was simply a stretch of rocky greenish ground, with patches of red vegetation. Here and there tall, red-needled trees, like weird pines, blocked the view. The atmosphere around was misty. The whole scene was in stark contrast to that outside the dome.

Did the intelligent race prefer to live in such a back-to-nature setting? Why should a titanic dome, the product of super-science, enclose a queer bit of pastoral scenery? Was it a park perhaps, or some sort of a playground?

York found no answer as he trudged halfway around the dome. It was all the same inside, and apparently untenanted. That was most puzzling of all. But suddenly he saw movement. He strained his eyes through the distortions of the transparent medium.

Two furry creatures were slinking among a group of trees, within a half-mile of York's position. He could barely make them out as apelike, walking erect on two legs. Their heads were remarkably large, denoting intelligence. Hand in hand, male and female apparently, they stumbled along. They glanced back at times, as though being stalked.

Abruptly another form lunged from behind a patch of red-berried bushes. It was a monstrous form, blubbery of body, revoltingly naked. Little stumpy legs moved it forward lumberingly. It had no claws. Its small head, bearing two saucer eyes, was perched on a long serpentine neck, giving it a periscopic view in all directions.

It looked, somehow, like a cross between a snake and walrus. It was repulsively ugly, but not formidable.

York watched as the two ape beings caught sight of the monster and ran with obvious fear. The beast lumbered after them clumsily. York, unconsciously loyal to the two beings more like himself, breathed in relief for them. They could easily outrun the horror.

But strangely their steps faltered. As though they had run into an invisible lake of syrup, they slowed down, their bodies straining futilely. At last the ape-man faced about, flinging the woman creature behind him. He awaited the attack of the monster.

"The ape-man will win," York told Vera by telepathy, having transmitted the episode. "The monster, though large, has no claws, or biting jaws, or any air of strength. The ape-man should have faced it in the first place. One twist of his powerful hands on that long, thin neck and he can tear the beast's ridiculous head off. The beast is the one who should run."

The ape-man, as though under York's orders, leaped forward to grasp the thin neck with his gorilla-like hands. But again something clogged his efforts. His arms fell helpless. He stood rigid. He made no move to escape as the beast whipped out a rubbery tentacle, wrapped it around his neck, and choked him lifeless. Then the tentacle's end probed into the corpse like a proboscis, and drained the dead ape-man to a bloodless husk.

Chapter 3

Anton York tried to break his gaze from the revolting scene. He saw the woman-creature stalk forward like a robot and submit herself to the choking tentacle and draining of blood.

With a final effort, York wrenched his eyes away. In the act, he knew why it was so hard.

"Hypnosis!" he breathed. "That horrible monster fascinates his prey as a snake does a bird, and the victim is doomed."

"But why do the builders of the dome, who must be higher life-forms than the ape-creatures, allow that to go on?" Vera's telepathic tone was shocked, unbelieving.

"I don't know," returned York. "There's some amazing mystery behind this. The dome-builders might be those same aliens of the patrol ship. I just glimpsed another dome, Vera, a few miles away. I'm going to that one and find out what I can."

"Tony, I'm worried. There is a terrible menace in all this. Please come back!"

But Vera knew that her husband wouldn't. Quite aside from his own problems and danger, York's scientific curiosity had been aroused. He had never, in all their travels among strange worlds, left a mystery unsolved.

The second dome, when York arrived, was exactly like the first in size and shape, enclosing a space about ten miles in diameter.

But the scene inside was vastly different. The ground was sandy and speckled with clumps of oddly shaped cacti life. The air seemed thin and clear, with heat ripples streaming down from the peak of the dome, where a huge gleaming apparatus hung suspended.

York quickly discovered mangy, lean creatures similar to Earthly wolves. They loped after and caught smaller animals, in this cross-section of an alien desert.

Suddenly, from behind a towering rock formation, stabbed a hissing ray. It struck a wolf creature, electrocuting it. York stared as the wielder of the electric gun ran from concealment.

At first glance, York understood why its movements were stiff and awkward, why its skin glinted metallically. York knew it to be a silicon being, one with silicon atoms replacing those of carbon. Intelligence reposed in the flint-scaled face, though it was dead of expression.

The silicon-man took out a sharp knife and began slicing the carcass. With a flint he struck fire, feeding it with twigs of dried cactus. He rolled a strip of flesh in the sand, then toasted it over the fire, finally gobbling it down with relish. Within his stomach, York surmised, some strange chemistry of digestion replaced the carbon atoms in the flesh-food with silicon atoms from the sand "salt."

As the silicon-man began a second strip, there was an interruption. A large form ambled from behind the rocks. York had to look twice, for it was the same repulsive type of beast that had killed the two ape-creatures in the other dome!

It came forward confidently. The silicon-man heard its approach. He whirled about, drew his ray gun.

"Give it to him!" York found himself urging the silicon-man. "Shoot the beast down."

The crystal-man seemed to make every effort. His gun pointed and his body trembled, but no shot was fired. Eyes fastened on the beast's saucer orbs, he stood as rigidly as a statue. Hypnosis again! The beast seemed to give a silent signal. With what might have been a curse, the silicon-man picked up his knife, holstered his gun, and trotted away. He looked back once, shaking his fist in a manlike gesture, but with an air of helplessness.

The hypno-beast promptly inserted its sucking organ into the wolf creature's corpse and drained it dry of blood. It could not use the silicon-men as food. But it still had the demoniacal power of chasing them away from prey they had killed.

What was the answer to this amazing riddle? The hypno-beast in two domes, in two different environments, lorded it over other life forms. Why had the builders done this? They could be neither the ape-men, the silicon-men, nor the hypno-beast. For all had obvious shortcomings as beings of great intelligence.

Who were they? Where were they? Why had they built these domes? Were they the ones who also patrolled space?

Driven by the mystery, and suspecting a third dome, York scanned the horizon and spied not one, but two more. He struck out for the nearest. So impatient that he sidestepped for nothing, he bowled over pulpy trees and fragile ferns with his swinging arms. He left behind him a trail of trampled vegetation that was already regrowing behind him.

The third dome was identical with the others. He would have been startled if it weren't. And the scene within, as he expected, was totally different from the other two domes, and also from this planet's indigenous environment.

It was a cold setting, in the third dome. White snow lay over all, sprayed down at times from an apparatus suspended under the dome's peak. Hardy vegetation existed here that had the peculiar power of motivation, like animal life. Stubby rootlets slowly inched forward the low trees and bushes, seeking a nutritious spot in which to sink the feeding roots. Shaggy white forms, almost invisible against the white background, sneaked among the moving vegetation. It must be bitterly cold in there, far colder than any spot on Earth, perhaps duplicating the frozen wastes of Uranus' moons.

York stared, startled by something.

"Vera, listen as I describe—" When he had finished, he asked: "Does it remind you of anything?"

After a moment her psychic voice came back excitedly.

"Yes. It does sound exactly like the fifth planet of 61-Cygni, which we visited over a thousand years ago. But Tony, that was in our Universe! How could that exact setting be here?"

York made no answer. He was watching a scene within the dome. It had a larger scope than he had at first realized. A small city stood under one part of the shell overhang. Solid ice blocks and snow cement composed the square buildings, decorated artistically with shaped icicles and patterned snow crystals. York had seen the same structures on 61-Cygni, unless imagination had filled the gaps of memory after a thousand years. Water was the staple building material, with temperatures ranging far below zero at all times.

Such was the city. The inhabitants were squat quadrupeds, their four feet flattened smooth so they could glide over snow and ice on these natural skis. All other surfaces of their bodies were covered with fluffy, warm feathers. They were warm-blooded creatures. Their beaked heads held large, intelligent eyes.

At the moment, excitement reigned in the village of snowbird people. The males had collected on the flat roof tops, swinging around catapults of leather and wood. They knew nothing of smelting or metals in their low-temperature environment. The boiling point of water was to them the blast heat of a high temperature furnace.

The attack they prepared for came. York's snow-blinded eyes hadn't even noticed the body of white forms rushing across the open stretch before the village. They were of the same race. York cursed, as he had always cursed over the civil wars of the human race.

The catapults thumped, slinging blocks of hard ice upon the attackers. The latter stood their ground, setting up giant catapults of their own. Great bombs of hard, crushing ice arced into the village, cracking through walls and ceilings.

The attackers were numerous, the besieged few. Perhaps this was the final assault of a long series of battles. The patched village crumbled, and the defenders were decimated under the bombardment.

York knew that hours had passed. He had watched with a fascinated wonder. In what way did this little battle, in a ten-mile patch of winter-world under a dome, fit in with the general mystery?

And then York saw the finale. From the distance, where they had been concealed by a mound of snow, came a group of naked hypno-beasts! No extreme of environment seemed to bother them. They passed among the victorious attackers, who advanced robotlike into the village. This was hypnosis control on a large scale. The hypno-beasts had directed an army of the bird people against the bird people's own kind! The beast-masters browsed through the village, probing their tentacles into dead bird-men, feeding well of victims killed by their own brethren.

York ground his teeth in loathing and rage at the hypno-beasts. Surely in all the two universes, there could not be a more revolting, dangerous form of life. For a mad moment he beat with his gauntleted fists at the transparent wall that separated him from the monsters, as though to charge in and challenge them. The shell felt as solid and unshakable as foot-thick steel.

"Tony, control yourself!"

York relaxed. "Vera, there's some answer to this. I won't give up. I'm going to the next dome—and the next—"

Three days passed. York again went sleepless and without food, drawing on the super-vitality with which the elixir of immortality had endowed him. He visited a dozen more domes.

In those dozen domes were the environments of a dozen different worlds. The creatures who roamed within ranged from wormlike crustaceans to great, scaly dinosaurian forms. Intelligence reposed in anything, from a dog-sized spider to a ten-foot high mammoth.

In one dome, blobs of liquid life were held together by thin skins. Rolling through a noisome, swampy purgatory, they devoured everything after spraying out a vicious poison whose touch was fatal.

Most of the intelligence levels were low, held back by inhibiting environments. But in one dome, tailed and fine-fingered beings had mastered a great science. Here too was civil war, with most of the beings dominated by the hypno-beasts, slowly conquering the rest.

The hypno-beast was in every dome! It was the sole common denominator of the baffling mystery. But what could be the purpose of the builders?

Trudging to the next dome, a queer phenomenon overtook York. With the suddenness of a dream ending, the flimsy life forms of the planet faded away. York watched the horizons melt down, as all the vegetation went to seed, dried to brittle dust. He looked up. The Cepheid sun had passed its maximum. Temperature was declining rapidly, and the short "winter" was approaching.

In the space of a few hours, the planet's surface was bare, wind-swept, as he had first seen it. He was on a high knoll, and when he looked around, he gasped. Within his range of vision now were dozens—no, hundreds—of the domes, in all directions. They marched down the horizons as though beyond them were hundreds more.

York was suddenly struck by something vaguely familiar in the sight. He squinted his eyes so the wide sweep of the planet below and the sky above were narrowed.

"Vera!" he telepathed excitedly. "I think I know now, partially. This is like a vast laboratory. Those domes are bell jars, in some stupendous series of experiments. The dome builders are the scientists. The creatures within are guinea pigs of this macro-cosmic research!"

"That sounds logical, Tony," Vera returned. "But for what purpose? And why should there be hypno-beasts in every dome?"

York pondered.

"The answer might be simpler than we suspect. The builders must be super-scientists, greater than any we've yet met. I am not excluding the Three Eternals and ourselves. They have roamed all through this universe, carrying back 'samples' of various worlds. Like biologists breeding cultures of mice or fruit-flies, they are carrying out a tremendous observation of hundreds of life forms. This must have taken centuries. The purpose behind it must be something vital to them. What can it be? Hundreds of life forms from all over their universe, pitted against the frightful hypno-beasts—"

"From our Universe, too!" interposed Vera. "I remember that winter-world of sixty-one Cygni clearly. The one under the third dome you visited was from there. Tony, what does it all mean?"

York had now approached the next dome.

He glanced in. Again he gazed upon an alien scene. Leafy green trees dotted a woodland sward of rich emerald grass. The air above was blue. Puffs of soft clouds drifted down from an apparatus at the dome's peak.

Not far beyond, a field of golden grain rippled as a warm breeze rustled over it. Several four-legged, homed and hoofed bovine creatures grazed on the grasses beside a brook that wound through sylvan glades. Little bright-colored birds piped from high branches, though York heard no sound through the transparent shell. A red-furred animal crept forward and suddenly leaped. A startled white-furred creature bounded away like a rabbit—

"Tony, don't you recognize it?" Vera's psychic voice was tense, as she read his transmitted description. "It's our own Earth!"

Chapter 4

York jerked violently. He had been staring impersonally, as he had at all the other alien environments, without realizing it was shockingly familiar. The blind spot in his brain had suddenly been dissolved.

"Vera, you're right!" His telepathic voice was a whisper. "It's a ten-mile section of our own native world, down to the last blade of grass. Good Lord, if there are Earth people here, and hypno-beasts also—"

Abruptly York's whole perspective changed. Before he had been scientifically fascinated, altruistically enraged at the dominance of the hypno-beast in each dome over races with which he felt no kinship. Now the hot blood pounded in his veins. In here must be his own people, his own kind. The race that had given him birth. The people with whom, though he was half a god above them, he felt the ties of blood brotherhood.

"The builders!" he shouted aloud in his suit, stunning his own ears. "Where are they? I must find them. They can't do this—"

He broke off. Something within the dome had caught his eye.

A man and a girl emerged from the shadowy forest, scaring away what York now recognized as a fox and a rabbit. They peered carefully in all directions and then advanced into the field, toward the cows. The man carried two empty buckets. Over his shoulder was slung a riflelike weapon, and in his belt was an unsheathed knife. Both were dressed in hides and woolens. The setting was pastoral, very near to the ancient pioneering days of America in the remote nineteenth century.

York knew nothing of those days personally. Earth for two thousand years had advanced to a much more scientific civilization. But the scene struck chords of aching kinship. This was a part of Earth, no matter if from a far past, and those two were his own people. If he could talk with them, they might explain this incredible mystery.

He pounded on the glass of the dome with his gauntlets and shouted, hoping to attract their attention. They were within a few hundred feet, but they took no notice. York desisted. Perhaps the dome was so polarized that they could see nothing but a blank gray wall.

York watched.

The couple reached the cows. The girl began milking, while the young man stood on guard, peering about cautiously. But gradually he became lax. His eyes wandered toward the girl herself. He spoke to her, smiling, and she smiled back. At times they laughed and he bent over once to touch her hair.

* * * *

The love of a man and a maid— It was here, too, under this prisonlike dome, on an alien world, in an utterly strange universe.

"Tony, it's wonderful and it's horrible," Vera said. "Wonderful that love can survive any twist of space and time, but horrible that these two have been taken from their home world. Do you suppose the builders watch somewhere, through some instrument, as if at ants?"

"Hush!"

York spied a slinking form among a patch of trees at the edge of the pasture. It was another man. He had unslung his rifle. He was kneeling now, taking aim for the man beside the girl.

York pressed his face against the dome glass and searched back of the man. He saw it suddenly, the pink-skinned, oily bulk of a hypno-beast. The man kneeling and shooting was under the beast's dominance, ready to kill at his bidding!

York screamed in warning. Then, realizing the uselessness of that, he concentrated on hurling a powerful telepathic warning. In all his wanderings throughout the universe, he had never yet heard of a substance that could stop the super-penetrative radiations of thought. But the dome did. His psychic vibrations rebounded with such force that they stunned his mind like a sledge-blow.

Yet perhaps the tiniest of thought impulses wormed through. The young man beside the girl turned uneasily, gripping the stock of his rifle. That move saved him for the time being. The shot ripped through the air from the ambusher, grazed his shoulder. Instantly he ducked, shouting to the girl. She flung herself flat in the grass, overturning the milk. The two cows lumbered away, lowing in fright at the sharp report. York filled in the sound sequences in his own mind.

Flat on his stomach, the young man unlimbered his rifle and cautiously raised his head, searching for his enemy. A puff of smoke from behind a bush and a shot that grazed over him gave him the clue. He fired back. A dozen shots were exchanged. One or the other was marked for death.

York ground his teeth when a shot from the attacker struck. In agony the young man doubled up, forming a better target. A second shot mercilessly crashed through his head. He sprawled out in death. The girl leaped up and flung herself on the body, weeping. Then she sprang to her feet and ran, as the victor came racing up, evidently to capture her alive.

Blindly the girl ran toward the dome shell. The man had cut her off from the concealing forest. Back of them the hypno-beast, who had instigated the tragedy, waddled up to the corpse. It occupied itself with its vampirish meal, as its brothers had over and over again in the other domes.

The girl was trapped. She ran to the dome wall and beat against it with her tiny fists, screaming. York moved to the spot. He saw her clearly, but she obviously saw nothing beyond the wall. She did not see that York stood there nearly mad with helplessness and fury. He could not answer the girl's pitiful cries for help.

She turned her back to the shell as the man came up. He was young, too, not vicious in appearance at all. But behind his youthful features was the mark of mental slavery. He was the living zombie of the hypno-beast. He spoke to her, and his face was strangely gentle.

York, no more than ten feet away outside the wall, was able to read their lips.

"Mara, why do you run from me? You loved me once. Come with me to our village."

"Yes, I loved you once," returned the girl, looking at him in pity rather than fear. "But now you are a slave of the Beasts. And you killed Jorel ruthlessly."

"But only at the command of my master. I did not want to." His eyes were pained and pleading. "Forgive me, Mara, and come to live with me. You did not love Jorel. What else have we to look forward to, save a little happiness, in this tiny world of ours?"

The girl's eyes blazed. "Why did you not kill the Beast, Mantar? Look, he squats there, unsuspecting. Shoot him!"

"I cannot!" The man shook his head.

"Mantar—for me!"

He looked at her and suddenly his face grew determined. Whirling, he flung up the rifle, taking aim at the feeding bulk a hundred yards away. It was a large target. He couldn't miss. York's heart leaped in hope, as the girl's must have.

But before a shot rang out, the beast's serpentine neck twisted. Its saucer eyes turned hypnotically on them, as though it kept mental tab on its slave. Mantar made a tremendous effort to press the trigger. His whole body trembled. But with a groan he lowered the weapon. The girl attempted to seize it, to do it herself. Now Mantar, under dominance, resisted her.

"I cannot," he said wearily. "I've tried before. All of us at the slave village have tried before. We cannot break that horrible power the Beasts have over our minds." He turned to the girl. "Mara, run! You are of the fortunate ones who can resist. Run for the forest. I think I can resist my master's mental command long enough to let you escape. Hurry!"

He gave her a push. But the girl turned back, and flung her arms around his neck.

"I can't. I still love you, Mantar. I will give you what happiness I can. I will go with you."

"No, Mara. It means slavery. Go, please."

But the girl clung to him. Then it was too late. The Beast left its ghoulish feast and advanced. Arm in arm, the pair walked toward it, to return with it to the slave village. On their young faces was written the bitterness of their chained lives under this dome lighted by an alien Cepheid sun.

York turned away as if from an unreal drama on some dream stage. Tears of helpless rage misted his eyes. Two thousand years of travel and observation among many civilizations had not made him callous to the fundamental decencies of life.

"It's awful, Vera," he said dully. "If I were in my own Universe, I'd blast down this dome on the spot and wipe those Beasts out to the last cell. Here I'm helpless even to get in." A determined note rang in his psychic tone. "But I will get in. I'll come back to the ship and conquer this universe's science laws, no matter how long it takes. And then—"

He was interrupted.

Over the bulge of the glass dome appeared a small ovoid ship. It swept down swiftly, darting back and forth as though searching. Instantly wary, York stood stock-stiff. Movement would betray him.

But the occupant of the craft seemed to spy him. It dropped down lightly and landed a dozen yards away. A hatch opened and a figure stepped out. In its hand glinted what could only be a weapon.

"Tony, what's wrong?"

"Silence, Vera," shot back York. "Don't contact me again unless you get my signal. On your life!"

Obediently no telepathic sound came from Vera.

York transferred his attention to the visitor. He was a travesty of a man, with spindly legs and arms, thin flat-chested body, and delicate tentacular fingers. Sharp, shrewd features peered inquisitively. Wearing no space-suit, he seemed perfectly at home in the bitter cold that York could not have survived for a minute. He breathed the hydrocarbonous air without discomfort. The forehead was low, topped by feathery hair, but the cranium in back bulged grotesquely. Intellect supreme reposed there.

"Who are you?" he demanded, in the universal language of telepathy. He answered himself. "You are obviously one of the J-X-Seventy-seven creatures. Earthmen, you are called. I was up in the conditioning apparatus when I thought I heard a powerful telepathic shout, and came to investigate. How did you get out of the dome?"

The being's canny eyes looked at York suspiciously.

"Or did you come from Earth? A ship from Earth was recently intercepted. I thought I heard you exchange a telepathic message with someone. Have you an accomplice? Where is your ship?"

Staccato, peremptory questions, they were just like those shot at the Three Eternals, before they were destroyed.

York faced a dilemma, greater than any before. If he revealed the true story, the ship would be found, Vera captured. Both would then be helpless.

York would have no chance to piece out the new science of this universe. He would have no future chance to face them, armed and powerful. These thoughts that flashed through his mind, he willed in a closed circuit, so the alien would not hear. There was only one solution.

"I have no ship," he returned in broadcast telepathy, knowing Vera would also hear. "I was in the dome. I built this space-suit, hoping to escape. Somehow, a few minutes ago, the dome wall where I sought an opening suddenly weakened and I fell through. I don't understand it. It simply happened." York held his breath. Only one thing made the thin story plausible. The dome must be an energy shell, not a matter shell. This York knew from the fact that his telepathy had not penetrated it. Matter was utterly transparent to thought. Therefore, if at times the energy shell could conceivably weaken in spots, one might fall through.

The being eyed him closely, suspiciously, but also with a certain disdain. It was not worth his continued attention.

"Come," he said. "Back you go. You won't be lucky enough to fall out a second time."

He extracted a queer, flaring-ended instrument from his belt and trained it on the section of the dome wall nearest them. Some force sprayed out in a six-foot circle, neutralizing the dome force. A push sent York through, along with a rush of hydrocarbonous air.

When he turned, he saw only a dull gray wall, blocking off all view of the outside world.

Chapter 5

He turned. He was within the dome, in the transplanted patch of Earth. He knew no more than before of the scheme behind it all. But some of the people here might furnish clues.

He stepped forward eagerly. Only one thing bothered him—his completely severed connection with Vera. Within himself he prayed that she would not foolishly wander from the ship and into danger.

For now he knew that danger supreme lurked behind all this.

He walked a hundred feet before he thought of removing his suit. He slung it over his shoulder and went on. He drew in deep lungfuls of air that had all the peculiar tang and sweetness of Earth's atmosphere. The builder-scientists had done a remarkable job of duplicating the Earth environment. It was pleasantly warm.

For awhile, wandering through a cool forest in which birds sang and squirrels chattered, York lost himself in a pleasant sense of well being, after the irksome period in the clumsy space-suit.

The sleep that he had long denied himself conquered him. He lay down in a soft patch of grass, passing off into restful slumber.

He awoke at a soft touch on his cheek.

Startled, he looked up into the face of a girl. It was a lovely face whose blue eyes and warm smile seemed meant only for him. The girl sat beside him, apparently having been there for quite awhile.

"What is your name?" she asked. "I am Leela. I watched you sleeping. You are good to look at."

York understood, though the words were a form of English queerly slurred.

"Anton York," he returned, trying to ease his archaic accent to something approaching hers.

The name that would have made any contemporary citizen of Earth freeze into awe and incredulous wonder failed to bring more than a welcoming smile to the girl's lips.

"An-ton Y-york," she repeated. "Anton York. I like it. And you are nice. I love you!"

Without another word she threw her arms around his neck, kissing him. York gasped at the girl's directness and pushed her away gently.

"Just a minute," he objected, and for perhaps the first time in centuries, he stammered a little. Fleetingly he felt glad that the wall of force kept Vera from knowing about the kiss. "Certainly you don't mean what you say—"

"But I do," insisted the girl softly, kissing him again. "Don't you want me to love you?"

York had to think for a moment. And for a moment he glanced around dizzily, aware that the girl's presence made the setting seem almost a paradise. Then his eyes caught a glint of pink skin a dozen yards away, behind leafy bushes.

Instantly the camouflage that had made the place seem so wonderful vanished. It was in reality a hell, in which the hypno-beasts not only played man against man, but woman against man!

York pushed the girl away. The monster, divining that it had been seen, lumbered forward. Over York swayed the serpentine neck and gleaming eyes of the Beast, reminding him of all the tragedies he had seen, in this dome and the others.

York sprang erect. Their eyes locked.

York's first impulse was to dash at the monster and twist its thin neck. But when he tried, he had the sensation of plunging into an invisible flood of force that tore at him and beat him back. It came from those glittering saucer eyes—the hypnotic force!

York tried to wrench his eyes from the Medusa stare that turned him to helpless stone, but failed. He fought the intangible force for a stubborn minute before he eased back.

Still he could not tear his eyes away. Now the force changed. Like a resistless gravity, it pulled him forward, but at the same time locked his arm muscles. He fought to strain backward against the ghostly hands that seemed to draw him forward. One step—two steps— He advanced like a bird caught in the spell of a snake.

The dome, trees, grass, girl—all had vanished. York saw only two enormous, deadly, compelling eyes that seemed to grow and fill the whole universe. He did not even see the quivering tentacle that stretched in anticipation for his throat.

But all the while, within York, something had been working. His subconscious mind gave the call of alarm. His immortality radiogens, stored with cosmic energy that constantly battled the poisons of old age and the raids of deadly germs, released a tide of power to his brain.

York stopped, stiffening, fighting the invisible force with renewed strength. The hypnotic force gave one final tug. York swayed, straining, and then took a step backward.

The spell snapped like the twang of a bowstring. York had won.

He leaped forward, but now in command of himself. The Beast bleated in fear, trying to run. York easily overtook it, grasped the neck and wrung it like that of a chicken. The head drooped on its broken neck. The hellish eyes glazed. The body thrashed wildly for several minutes before it finally lay still in death.

York stared at it with hands on hips, panting more in loathing and rage than exertion. Never in all his exploits had he felt more completely satisfied. He had destroyed a fleet of powerful ships once, and moved worlds, and wielded a godlike science. But here with his bare hands he had killed a repulsive beast. That was his supreme achievement!

After awhile, he smiled in detached calm at the strange contrast between this event and the others in his stirring career. His thoughts were terminated by a pair of soft arms that stole about his neck.

"You have saved me—freed me!" Leela murmured. "Now I truly love you. Take me with you."

York disengaged himself firmly.

"Leela, I have a wife. I've had her for a long, long time and wouldn't change now!"

He wondered what she would say if he told her he was two thousand years old. He decided not to, for the present.

"You have a—mate?"

"Yes." York was relieved, for she did not press her attention. "Now tell me about this beast, and you." To himself he mused: "Beauty and the Beast."

"The master brought me here, where the Free Ones often come. If we found a young man—as we did you—I was to lure him with me, away from any others. It was a hateful duty, please believe that. Then the Beast would either kill him or bring him back to be a slave. The Beasts use all sorts of means to reduce the numbers of the Free Ones. They are trying to kill off all those of the Free Ones who are too mind-powerful to become slaves."

"You mean there are certain ones here who can resist the Beasts' spell, like myself?"

The girl looked at him, puzzled.

"Surely you know that. Why do you ask questions as though you have never been here before?"

"I haven't," York said. "I came from outside the dome wall."

She stared at him in sudden astonishment, at his strange clothes, at his oddly glowing eyes, the sign of immortality. After a moment, shrugging helplessly, she answered his questions.

"Yes, many can resist the spell. And each generation there are more."

"Generation!" gasped York. "You've never heard of me, Anton York? You've never been on Earth?"

"Earth? You mean the Original World, which our forefathers came from, they say. No, of course not. I was born here."

"And how many generations have there been, according to that story?"

"One hundred."

One hundred generations! At least two thousand years! For twenty centuries Earth people had been under this great dome, living and dying, in some gigantic experiment carried out by the dome builders. York shook his head. More and more it loomed as something vital and far reaching—and sinister.

"Do you know why this was done?" he pursued. "Why your forefathers were taken from the Original World and brought here? Or where the hypno-beasts came from?"

"I know little," vouched the girl. "But perhaps at the village of the Free Ones some of the learned men know. Come, I'll lead you there."

Glancing at him in growing wonder, she turned. York followed.

The way led out of the small forest, into open land. There were more grazing lands for cattle and beyond lay a checkerboard of tilled fields with ripening crops. Nut-brown men labored among them and waved greetings. They all had rifles and looked cautiously behind York and Leela to make sure they were not slaves of the hypno-beasts, on some sinister errand.

The village two miles ahead struck a chord of ancient memory in York's mind. It was a stockaded camp, surrounded by a wall of high wooden posts with here and there a lookout station. Within were log cabins and horse-drawn wagons and buckskin garbed people. It was a setting that had vanished from Earth's history since the nineteenth century. It was here, reincarnated and apparently jelled. Why?

York's mind bristled with unanswered questions. He was impatient when an elderly woman spied them. She dropped an armload of kindling wood and hugged Leela.

"My child, my child!" she cried, yet with a stoic lack of tears in her motherly joy. "You are back. I thought I'd never see you again. It's been a year. Leela, my baby—"

"He rescued me." Leela pointed to York. An eager crowd formed around, shouting greetings to the girl who had miraculously returned from the slavehood of the Beasts. "He killed my Beast master with his bare hands!" She told the story.

The crowd gaped at York in awe. As much, York mused, as the peoples of the thirty-first century had gaped at him for moving worlds. Here he had done nothing more than wring a Beast's neck. He hadn't used a single scientific principle except that a broken spine caused death.

York made an impatient gesture and the girl understood. She led him to the center of the village where a two-storied cabin stood, guarded by two long-haired stalwarts with rifles. One of them started and greeted Leela with a hug and kiss. York smiled at her hungry response. It relieved him entirely of his role as hero-rescuer, with which she had girlishly surrounded him.

The young man stuck out his hand, after the story, and wrung York's hand with a grip of steel. No weaklings, these men. Then he spoke hesitantly.

"According to custom, Leela is yours."

"But I have a mate," York returned quickly. "She is outside the dome wall." He began to explain. Seeing their blank stares, he asked again for an audience with those in authority.

"You mean the Congress." The young guard went in and returned after a moment, nodding. "They will see you."

The Congress proved to be a group of ten elderly, gray-haired men, past the days of physical activity but wise in years and experience. They listened as Leela once again gave the details.

"It is a strange story," said Robar, the head of the council. "Who are you, Anton York? I have never heard the name York among our people." There was suspicion in his voice, and in all their stares. "You may be from the Beast village, sent as a spy! The Beasts try all sorts of tricks in their attempt to subdue us."

The atmosphere became tense, and the young guard even raised his gun threateningly.

"No!" It was Leela who sprang to York's defense. "Don't forget I was in the Beast village for a year. The name is not known there, either. If he is a spy, so am I, for I came from the Beasts."

The impassioned words served to heighten the tension, included the girl in their suspicions. York stepped forward with determination.

"Listen to me. I have lived for two thousand years. I was born on what you know as the Original World, in the twentieth century. In the year seventeen-seventy-six, thirteen colonies in a land called America declared their independence from a land across the Atlantic Ocean. They formed a Congress. Your Congress comes from that. In the following century, the thirteen colonies grew, pushing westward against redmen called Indians. Eventually the land stretched from ocean to ocean. There was a Civil War, the assassination of a great man named Lincoln. Then an industrial empire arose, oil was found, gold. A steam railroad spanned the continent. Buffalo herds were exterminated."

Excitement grew in the men's faces.

"It fits in with our legends," whispered Robar. "The thirteen American tribes—the redmen—the Big War—buffalo vanishing." He looked at York with sudden awe. "I believe you, Anton York. You have come from the Original World to help us?"

"If I can," York nodded. "But first I must know all I can. What do your legends tell of coming here?"

Robar pondered, as though searching misty impressions handed down from father to son.

"Little. Until eighteen-eighty-eight, our forefathers lived on the Original World, in a village like this, called Fort Mojave. They fought the redmen at times. But one day strange flying ships appeared, against which their guns were useless. The whole village of a thousand men, women and children was forcibly taken here. At first there were no Beasts. They lived with little trouble, though sad at being taken for their home world. Then the Beasts appeared suddenly, and life became a constant battle against them. So it has been for generations."

"But why were they brought here?" York queried. "And why were the hypno-beasts introduced into this bit of transplanted Earth?"

"It was never known. Not one glimpse of those mysterious people is recorded. Life has gone on, as it must. We have almost come to forget how it all started. All we concern ourselves with is the survival against the Beasts."

York bit his lips. The mystery was still unexplained. The dome builders had not vouched one item of information to their bell jar specimens. Nor, probably, to any of the other kidnapped beings in all the other domes.

Rage shook Anton York. It was cold-blooded, autocratic, cruel if not actually vicious—this experimentation with generations upon generations of poor, marooned groups of beings. Something must be done!

Chapter 6

In the following days, York found out all he could ever find out, under the dome itself. The village of the Free Ones housed about six thousand people. Their fields and hunting ground occupied a little more than half of the total space under the dome. Beyond a narrow river that bisected the area was the territory in control of the hypno-beasts and their mental slaves. It was understood that the slaves numbered about four thousand. But their life-span was short, for the Beasts bred them as food.

In all, then, there were ten thousand human beings under the dome, in this isolated bit of Earth. That meant over three hundred persons per square mile, more crowded than Europe had been before the scientific era of soil-less crops! Under those circumstances, waging a grim battle against the Beasts constantly, science had not had a chance to advance. The few deposits of metal ores and important minerals had long since been worked out. Metal was hoarded like gold.

York's observations included the river. It sprang from underground, near one dome wall, and vanished underground again at the opposite side. A thousand feet above, under the center of the dome, he could vaguely see the giant, gleaming apparatus that duplicated sunlight in regular twenty-four hour periods. At times it puffed out clouds, showers and even fogs. Outside the dome was a hydrocarbon atmosphere, a climate ranging from Uranian cold to Mercurian heat under a variable Cepheid sun. In here was a bit of Ireland or California.

The builders had done a perfect job. But why? The question rang like a gong in York's mind. And gradually he came to have the feeling of being watched. He sensed eyes above that looked down, coldly and scientifically, watching over all and recording the pulse of life beneath. It was a maddening sensation.

York felt like screaming at times, though for two thousand years he had learned to control his emotions with almost godlike equanimity. The other people had come to accept dome life as normal, natural, and all else as illusion or legend.

York temporarily shelved the matter of the grand purpose behind all this. The immediate problem was the hypno-beasts. If he could do something against them, he would perhaps be foiling in some small way the scheme of the master-scientists.

One horrible thought lurked in his mind. Suppose the dome builders were propagating the hypno-beasts for the eventual purpose of dominating the universe with them?

"We hope to conquer the Beasts in due time," Robar informed him. "In each generation a higher percentage of the children are almost completely immune to the Beasts' hypnotic powers. For the first thousand years, the village of Free Ones was small and barely escaped extinction hundreds of times, but in the past thousand years our numbers have increased. Today we outnumber the slave group. In another few centuries—"

"Too long to wait," York interrupted. "The hypno-beasts are semi-intelligent, but not scientific. Science can destroy them. How do your guns operate?"

Examination proved that the rifles were models of the flint-lock muskets of the nineteenth century. The bullets were of hard wood, to conserve metal. The propellant was powdered charcoal. Because of the peculiar laws of this universe, the mere firing of a pinch of charcoal had the power of guncotton, as York's rocket had worked with slow-burning phosphorus.

"There's some all-embracing equation behind it all," York told himself. "If I could only find it, I'd have the power to wipe out the Beasts, blast down the dome, and face the master race—"

A horn sounded, on this third day. It was the alarm of attack. Instantly the village mobilized. Men marched to the river, York with them. The enemy troops had crossed in wooden boats and now lay scattered behind bushes and low hills. The Free Ones took to cover and it settled down to sniping.

York, with a rifle resting in a tree crotch, could not bring himself to fire at the figures he sighted now and then. They were human, after all, even if bent on killing their own kind under the command of the hypno-beasts. The Beasts were there, across the river, directing their forces by long-range hypnosis. York could feel the subtle pull of it.

The sniping dragged on for hours, till the Free Ones flanked and drove the attackers back. They did a revolting thing. Hoisting their dead to their shoulders, they deposited them on the other bank, at the feet of the Beasts, who then fed. That seemed to be the sole purpose of the attack, unless it was revenge for the beast killed by York.

The opposing forces left the river bank and vanished toward their village. The short battle was over. York watched as the Free Ones went among their dead and cut them in ribbons so that all the blood drained into the ground. The grisly business was done stoically. In the curious economy of the little patch of Earth, it served to foil any chance of the Beasts feeding on them, and it also fertilized the ground.

Back in the village, York found the girl Leela standing among the wounded. She bravely choked back tears as she stared down at her lover's white face.

"He will live," she whispered. "But he will never walk again. He was paralyzed by a shot in the spine. Oh, Anton York, can't you help me?"

She was suddenly weeping against his shoulder. York patted her soothingly, and then set his lips.

"Do you want to take a chance?" he asked her. "A chance that he will be whole again—or die?"

"I trust you, Anton York," the girl said instantly.

He operated. Centuries before, against the day when some physical accident might try to rob him of Vera, York had studied surgical technique and become adept. With a skill that no Earthly surgeon had ever approached, he removed the bullet with a sharp knife. Antiseptic herbs that the people cultivated protected the wound. The young man passed into a restful sleep from which he would awake fully restored.

York waved aside the girl's gratitude and shook a fist up toward the peak of the dome. Within him, rage had become a tidal force. They were playing at being gods up above, the merciless dome builders, unmoved by these tragedies.

They *must* be out to conquer the universe, breeding the horrible hypnobeasts as their scavenging horde! And it must be stopped.

But how? York, super-scientist of Earth's Universe, would have tried. But York, science-less orphan in a new, unknown universe, was practically helpless.

A year passed. York spent most of his time with endless computations. For a blackboard he used a patch of sand and a stick. Again and again he laboriously worked out equations for the new universe's master laws, only to find, by simple tests, that they were wrong. All the while he had the feeling of being watched. And to worry him further, what had become of Vera? Had she run out of food or air supplies? Had she been captured?

One day she seemed near him. He shrugged off the hallucination, but suddenly jumped up. It was her mental voice crying, faint and far away. York followed it like a radio beam and came to a portion of the dome wall where it was strongest.

"Vera!" he telepathed. Most of his mental vibration surged back from the wall, but some leaked through. "Vera, are you there? We're taking a chance, contacting like this." Then he became tenderly eager. "Are you all right, my darling of the ages?"

"Yes, Tony. I can see you. You look thin and haggard. I had to come. I've been distilling the planet air, and eating the pulp of the twenty-two day plants. I'm all right."

York briefly recounted his year of separation from her.

"I'm all right, too, but I have to solve the master laws of this universe."

"Tony, that's why I came. I've been working on computations, also. It came to me suddenly. Entropy, Tony—This universe has a lower entropy. Exactly one point one-six-four. I measured it."

It struck fire in York's mind.

"That's it, Vera! Good girl. But now, go quickly before the dome people detect you. I'll work out the laws. I'll wipe out the hypno-beasts, and then break out of the dome, one way or another."

"Be careful, dear," with that, Vera's mental voiced moved away.

York returned to the village, his brain buzzing. Entropy, of course! Not only slower light slower sound and "longer" space, but also a slower entropy—slower dissipation of energy in this universe. It accounted for the relatively high potential energy in slow-burning fuels. This universe had not run down as much as Earth's Universe.

With this vital clue, York's equations began to take life. Formulas dovetailed, and the ubiquitous zero did not always crop up to mock him. In another month, he had calculated the elements of a ray weapon, freed of the clumsiness of propellant guns.

He called Robar and the Congress to session. The men looked at him a little strangely.

"What is it, Anton York?" Robar asked. "We are not sure if you are a madman or not. For a year you have spent your time hunched over a plot of sand, making marks with a stick. What have you been trying to do?"

"Discover science for you."

"Science? We do not even know the word."

York began at the beginning. "After the time of your forefathers, science arose on the Original World. Machines were made that do all things. Also weapons of war. Weapons, for instance, that blast things to bits. I am going to make one. I will need help and metals. Most of your rifles will have to be melted."

Robar looked dubious. "It will be dangerous partially to disarm ourselves. And how do we know that you are not merely a madman?"

The gods must be laughing at the irony, York thought. But he could not blame them. They knew nothing of him, or even of science. York picked up a little quartzite pebble that he saw on the floor.

"If I make this stone shine in the dark," he demanded, "will you agree?"

They nodded. York went out and returned with the radium capsule of his suit's heating coil. Radium and radioactivity were two things not greatly changed by the new universe's laws. Holding the radium point near the stone, it shone fluorescently in the dark. The councilors exclaimed in wonder. The project began.

York met and conquered what seemed insuperable difficulties in the next six months. Metals had different melting points in this universe, glass had altered properties, and electricity had new values for its ohm, ampere and volt. But at last he had a workable radium battery that shot its current through a series of interlaced coils behind a convex mirror of polished steel. The whole was mounted on a large-wheeled base.

It was heavy and clumsy, and so crudely worked that even an artisan of the late Stone Age might have laughed. But it held a giant of power.

At the final test, York clapped together the contact handles of his switch. Electricity pulsed through the coils. A field of strain surrounded a metal bar. Its end, at the focus, became a diamond of incandescence—and atomic disintegration. An energy ray of neutrons hissed from the cathode mirror. It stabbed invisibly for a lone tree which had been picked out as the target. The tree cracked in half, its mid-portion blasted to atoms.

The villagers cried aloud in fear and wonder, and their faces plainly said, "Witchcraft!" York wondered what they would say if they knew he had once, in his own Universe, moved the planet Mercury. Yet York himself was stirred by the simple blasting of the tree. It marked the first step in his conquest of the new universe's laws of science and power. Back in his ship's lab, if he could get there, he would be in a position to wield powerful forces—defy the dome builders!

But first, the hypno-beasts…

Chapter 7

M-Day reigned in the village. Every able-bodied male flocked to the banner. This was not to be a war, but a crusade against the hated Beasts. Once and for all, under this dome, they would be exterminated. As York led his two thousand grim, determined men, he had the curious thought that in any Earthly war they would be worth ten thousand other fighters. For in their breasts beat the tidal wave of hate nurtured for twenty centuries.

They crossed the river, most of them swimming, holding their rifles high. York's machine was pulled across on a raft. On the opposite shore, in enemy territory, sentry-line retreated till reinforcement came. In a matched battle, York's yelling men smashed through. They took prisoners wherever possible. For when the Beasts were gone, these poor mental slaves would again be free, normal humans.

The army marched on the Beast village. It was a sprawling, filthy mass of hovels, but suitably protected by a high wooden wall manned by riflemen. The approach was an open field. York's men could employ no strategy except to scatter and crawl forward from clump to clump of grass. Bullets whined, picking them off.

York gave his instructions to Darrill, Leela's young man, who was commander.

"Get your men as close to the wall as you can, without too much loss of life. Give me time to set up my machine and aim. Then rush in and mop up. Kill all the Beasts you can."

Darrill nodded and his men crawled forward, like the plainsmen of old stalking the wily Indian. York went over his machine's parts carefully, then aimed it for the nearest part of the city wall. He pressed the contact switch. His first blast went high, thundering harmlessly against the dome wall beyond.

His second struck. A ten-foot portion of the stockade burst into flying splinters. Two men, slaves of the Beasts, went with it as mere splinters of flesh. Again and again York knifed his switch, hurling detonations of neutrons, raking the village wall. It became a saw-edged ruin.

The village beyond was exposed to attack!

Now Robar's forces arose and charged. The Beasts, in their quasi-human cunning, rallied their slave-men to the breaches. They poured a withering fire at the attackers. York hated to do it, but he swept his super-machine-gun across the defenders' ranks. Slave-men and Beasts fell in bloody tangles.

Robar's forces reached the village, stormed in, and began mopping up. Since most of them were at least partially immune to the hypnosis, by heredity, they promised to make it short work.

York stood tensely. Why hadn't the dome builders interfered? He had half expected it. He was prepared to swing the snout of his super-gun up, if they appeared, and blast venomously at them. If they had some weapon ready at the dome's peak, and fired down, York would blast down the dome even if that meant a choking death.

It was a grim moment, for that was York's first challenge to the dome builders. But not a sign came from the mysterious watchers.

The Beasts in the village did not accept extermination so easily, however. York had not noticed what went on at the back of the village, where a stretch of concealing forest grew to the wall edge. He was suddenly aware of danger to himself. A force of hypno-beasts and about fifty slave-men were creeping up at his side.

Alone with his machine, York was surrounded. The men, at their masters' commands, raised their rifles. A fusillade of bullets would riddle York and shatter his machine. Whatever the outcome of the village battle, York would meet his end.

Death and Anton York stood face to face.

Was this the way in which the dome-scientists were retaliating? Were they controlling the Beasts as they controlled the slave-men, giving them the mental command to kill York?

York first darted his hand for the switch. At least he would take with him some of the enemy. A second thought clutched him. He had easily snapped, at first try, the hypnotic-power of the hypno-beast he had once met. Suppose he hurled the full power of his mentality at them now?

In his two thousand years of life, York had come to learn something of the limitless depths of power within the mind. He had at times used hypnosis himself, and telekinesis. He rang out a call now to the cosmic fed radiogens of his brain. A field of force radiated from him. His mental force met and challenged the combined mental force of the five hypno-beasts.

A strange, silent battle was being fought there.

One lone man stood rigid, surrounded by five repulsive, rigid Beasts. No physical movement betrayed the fact that between them had sprung mental forces of tremendous magnitude. The slave-men cowered, mere brawling pawns in this psychic war. Whichever won, York or the Beasts, would command the slave-men to kill the other.

Perhaps a second passed, perhaps ten minutes. York felt the growing strain. Sweat ran down his face. His brain seemed to be burning alive as his immortality radiogens poured their energy into the field of mental force. He could not stand it much longer. His brain would burn out like an overloaded generator.

The ending was curiously undramatic. One of the Beasts seemed to sigh suddenly. It toppled over, head drooping on its serpentine neck, Medusa eyes closing. It was through, burned out! Another followed, then two more.

The last held out. Its eyes locked with York's. York, reeling, called forth one more surge of mind energy.

The last beast toppled. With a snap, the spell broke.

"Shoot the Beasts," York commanded mentally.

Obediently the slave-men poured bullets into the fallen bodies. They jerked convulsively and died. York slipped to the ground, drained of energy, and fell into a state that was more of a coma than sleep.

When he came to, young Darrill was splashing water in his face.

"Anton York!" he cried joyfully. "The village is ours! We killed many of the Beasts. But about half escaped, running to the woods."

York pulled himself together.

"No time to lose," he said. "Organize a Beast-hunt. String your immune ones in a wide line and drive the Beasts into the open, past my machine. Every last one must be exterminated."

It took a week. The immune men, like beaters driving wild game past hunters, herded the panic-stricken hypno-beasts at will. Whenever they were in the open, York's neutron gun blasted into their numbers, ripping them to quivering shreds. It was not till Robar's men had roamed for twenty-four hours without finding a Beast that York nodded in satisfaction.

"There is not a single Beast left in this ten-mile patch of Earth," he announced.

But at the same moment, a lumbering form charged from a patch of bushes. It was the last of the Beasts. It seemed berserk, coming forward against a thousand rifles and the blasting-gun.

"Wait!" York yelled, as the men took aim with their guns. "Surround him. Bring him here alive."

A dozen men dragged the struggling, bleating creature before York. Hiding his loathing at its blubbery, oily body and snakelike head, York addressed it by telepathy.

"Can you understand me?" he queried. "Will you answer my questions?"

"I understand you," came back clearly from the hypno-beast, confirming York's belief in their semi-intelligence. "I will answer questions only if you promise me speedy death. I do not wish to live here, the last of my kind." York agreed. "Tell me this. Do you know why you are here, under a dome, pitted against Earth people?"

"No."

"You don't know why your kind have been put here, in hundreds of domes, pitted against hundreds of life forms?"

"I did not know of the other domes." The creature was obviously startled. "I wonder—" His thoughts trailed to nothingness.

"What is your native world?"

"The planet system of another sun, according to a legend of ours. I was born here, of course. A long time ago, our progenitors were brought here to this dome."

"And you have no idea why?"

"None. Now give me death."

York gave the signal and a fusillade of bullets snuffed out the life of the last hypno-beast under that dome. York looked up. Were the dome builders staring down, watching in mockery? His hatred and loathing of the Beasts swiftly transferred to them. Why hadn't they interfered? It must be against their plans to have the hypno-beasts wiped out under any one dome.

The maddening enigma of it grated York's nerves. Was he a pawn in their hands? Or would he have the chance yet to do something, before they were quite aware of who he was and what he planned? If he could only get to his ship!

York worked rapidly. He altered the adjustments of his machine so it would radiate sheer energy. The scientific laws of this universe were no longer a mystery to him. He had the machine dragged to one part of the dome wall, and donned his space-suit. Its oxygen unit still held a trickle of the life-giving gas.

He faced the people he had freed of an age-long menace. "I am leaving the dome. But I will be back soon, to free you and return you to Earth. I swear it."

He stepped through a patch of the energy wall, neutralized by his machine's counter energy. Like a god he vanished from their sight, as he had so often from the people back on Earth.

Beyond the dome wall, he crouched for a moment, quietly, warily. Would the dome builders pounce on him now, like a cat on a mouse? But nothing happened.

York left the dome, treading through a pulpy jungle. The Cepheid luminary was just at its periodic maximum, shining as a blue-hot sun. The outer coating of York's suit, a product of his advanced science, threw off waves of blistering heat.

He reached the ship, not daring to call Vera mentally before that moment He jerked the lever of the air-lock and rushed in.

"Vera!" he called vocally. "I'm back. Vera—"

There was no answering sound in the cabin. York ran through the storerooms and laboratory before he knew the truth. Vera was not there! At first he felt almost physically sick. Then York's nerves eased. Perhaps she had merely stepped out to gather pulp food. Guardedly he sent out a mental call, extending its range slowly in a widening circle about the ship. When no answer came, he recklessly swept a circle a hundred miles around.

Still there was no answer. Vera could not possibly be within range without answering—if she were alive.

York's eyes went bleak. There was only one answer. The dome builders had discovered the ship and captured Vera!

The icy rage that swept through York's veins at that moment would have made any of his past enemies—the fifty Immortals, Mason Chard, the Three Eternals—tremble in stark fear. No savage Stone Age man, losing his mate of a few years, could match the blazing agony that seared within York. Vera had been his love, his constant companion, for two thousand years.

York made a vow, in a cold, deadly voice.

"No matter what or who you are, dome builders, I'll search you out. And if you've touched a hair of her head—"

He could find no threat that was adequate.

Chapter 8

Anton York labored for a month. He feared detection at any moment. Why didn't the dome builders come back for him? Why hadn't the ship been guarded? The sheer strangeness of it utterly baffled him. Vera, of course, would never betray him. But by adding two and two, they must know of York. Were they so all-powerful that they feared nothing?

In that month, York accomplished miracles. He worked at his gravity engine, a protective screen against weapons, and his own weapons. Before, the ship had landed almost a derelict. Now it was again a floating fortress of might, as it had been in his own Universe.

It was not miraculous. It was simply that York had finally solved the new universe's master laws. It took only minor adjustments to fit his instruments and energy coils to work under those new principles. And by virtue of lower entropy—higher available energy—York's ship was now a more formidable fighting craft than it had been in Earth's Universe.

Seated at his controls, he raised the ship one day. Lightly as a feather it darted up. His energy coils drew power from the planet's gravity field, like a sponge sucking up water. As a test, he shot into space and rammed his ship forward at the speed of light. He braked with his inertia-less field to zero in three seconds, without feeling the slightest jar. The engines hummed smoothly, like a snoring giant.

As the test of his protective screen, he chased down a meteor and cracked into it at twice the speed of light. His screen shattered the huge stone instantaneously. His hull was untouched.

He chased down another meteor and turned his gamma-sonic weapon on it. The livid beam whiffed fifty millions of tons of matter away in twenty-five seconds. He was amazed himself. In his own Universe, where lower energies reigned, it would have taken at least twice that time.

Satisfied, he dropped back to the planet, hovering over the domes. He saw their full extent now. There was more than a thousand in all, occupying a good portion of the otherwise barren wastes.

York drew a deep breath. He felt better now, better than he had for the three years he had been in this universe. He was no longer a marooned, helpless being. At his fingertips again was super-power.

He pondered. What was he to do? How could he find the dome builders? And Vera? They seemed bent on ignoring him. He speculated the thought of searching the other twelve planets of the Cepheid sun. This one seemed to be merely an experiment station. Find their center and confront them—

York smiled suddenly. He had a better idea. Ignore him, would they? His hands moved to the controls. His little globular ship dropped toward a dome. York sprayed down energy neutralizing force and his ship dropped through the dome wall into its interior. The wall reformed back of him. He was within. This was the very first dome he had seen, with its pathetic aperace dominated by the hypno-beasts.

To the denizens of the dome, it must have seemed like the visitation of a god. The globular ship darted around like an angry wasp. Whenever a hypno-beast appeared, a ray stabbed down, and a puff of black soot replaced the Beast. In an hour, York had cleared the dome of every lurking hypno-beast. At the last, he hung over a crude village of the cowering, trembling ape-people, hurling down a mental message.

"You are free of your enemies! You will be returned to your home world eventually. I, Anton York, say it!"

This last was a challenge to the dome builders. From dome to dome York went. He freed the snowbird people of their hypno-beasts, and the silicon-men, telling both that they would be returned to their home worlds. Then he rocketed to other domes, raying down the hypno-beasts relentlessly. Intelligent they might be, and as deserving of their own existence as any other race. But their connection with the dome builders branded them, in York's mind, as inimical, only deserving extinction.

Dome after dome, and the hunt sang through York's veins lustily. This was the sport of the gods! But suddenly the cold shock of reason doused his mind. Another ship appeared before his, going from one dome to another.

Instantly York became cold, wary.

The dome builders had finally answered the attack he had made against their domes. He put his protective screen up to full power. No matter what weapons they had, he knew his screen would stand at least a few minutes of battering. He could flee, as a last resort, if his own weapon failed. Out in space he knew a hundred tricks for eluding pursuers. There was no immediate danger.

He had tensed himself for attack, but it did not come. Instead, from the lone ship, came the clarion voice of telepathy.

"You are Anton York, of Earth?"

"Yes. You have my wife, Vera, in captivity. My first demand is that you release her. Secondly, your dome experiment, whatever it is, must be stopped. The various races must be returned to their own worlds."

The psychic voice that came back seemed to be laughing.

"Indeed! You have appointed yourself champion of the universe, Anton York?"

"Call it what you want," York shot back. "I only know that those races are suffering. They have been for too long under the dominance of the hypno-beasts. The Beasts must be destroyed to the last one."

The other being seemed to stop laughing and became very sober.

"Exactly. And now we have found the way."

Startled, York almost bit his tongue.

"You mean you have *wanted* the Beasts destroyed? Your long, elaborate experiment is for that end? But why—"

"I will explain all. Come with me to our main world, the fifth planet."

"Wait! If this is trickery, I have a powerful weapon."

As answer, a tongue of queer green light suddenly sprang from the alien ship. It licked greedily around York's ship. His electro-screen melted away as though it were cotton. The tip of the green tongue flicked against the hull and gouged out a chunk of meteor-hard metal, with the ease of a whip flicking off a patch of human hide.

York felt it as a tremendous shock that jarred through every inch of the ship, as if a mountain had been hurled down on him. He gasped. His screen, against which great meteors at the speed of light would have cracked to powder, had been pierced as easily by the green ray as a knife going through butter.

Illimitable power! Gigantic might! These the alien must have.

York had to know the full bitter truth. He tripped the lever of his great gamma-sonic weapon, training it dead-center on the other ship. The blast that emerged would have bored a hole ten miles deep in solid steel. It crashed against the alien's screen, threw up a shower of sparks—and dissipated. It dissipated like vagrant smoke. York was helpless.

"You see?" came from the alien. "We are supreme scientists. Your puny screen would go down in an instant, if I used any amount of power. But your death is not wished. Up to now we've patrolled space against possible expeditions from any planet. But we no longer have to. Follow me."

York followed. They arose from the planet of domes and arrowed toward the Cepheid sun. Within an hour, at the speed of light they had neared the fifth planet. It was strangely like Earth, blue and cloud-wreathed. But only under the waning rays of the variable sun. Under its maximum rays, it must change to a hell-hot purgatory, ten times more trying to life than the fierce humidity of Venus.

"You live under domes, on your planet?" York queried, before they landed.

"No," came back promptly, politely. "We live in the open. Our whole evolution has been adjusted to the periodic change. We live in frigidity during the wane, and in superheat when our sun waxes, and it is all the same to us. It is the keynote, Anton York, of the story I will soon have to tell."

York's ship landed, after the alien's, in a wide field surrounded by a gleaming city that took his breath away. York had seen countless civilizations, but none so manifestly magnificent as this. He was aware of various subtle impressions. First, a vague air of sadness hung over the city. But it was an air of sadness that was lifting, like mist under a bright sun.

Also, he noticed several ships, in the huge spaceport, hovering as though awaiting their arrival. They dipped. York was not sure, but the ships seemed to be saluting him! The burning mystery of it all piled pyramid high in York's seething mind. In some way, York, or something he represented, was a hero to these people.

He stepped out in his space-suit, all thought of personal danger gone. The being from the other ship was like the one he had seen once before—thin, spindly, large-headed. His resplendent dress, of fine-spun metallic cloth, suggested high rank. By the deference of his crew and the others around, he must be of the highest rank.

"Yes, I am Vuldane," the being returned, catching York's thought. "King of our race, the Korians. Follow me to my palace. Your wife, Vera, is there."

York stepped eventually into a huge, glittering chamber. He saw only one thing, however. Vera stood in a space-suit ahead.

He crushed her in his arms. He couldn't say or telepath a word, at finding her safe.

"Tony, dear," she said. "I worried for you. But I knew you would be brought here safely."

She was amazingly calm. And behind her calmness was an odd, puzzled look. York looked around carefully. Suddenly he grasped her wrist. With his other hand he jerked a weapon from his belt, a smaller edition of his gamma-sonic force. He pointed it at Vuldane's unprotected chest.

"Vuldane," he snapped mentally. "I came here only to find my wife. Now, unless you want to die, command free departure for us from this planet. I'll talk with you in space, later, if you come in an unarmed ship. I'll give you three seconds."

The king stood rooted in surprise, though not fear. York counted three, then began to squeeze the trigger. But something knocked the gun down. It was Vera herself.

"Tony—no! It would do no good. They would hound you down. You must listen to their story first. And when it's done, you will wonder yourself what is right and what is wrong."

York holstered his gun. It had been a mad thing to do. But the past adventures, and the staggering mystery of it, had unbearably tortured his nerves. He whirled on the king, who seemed unperturbed.

"Tell me the story quickly. You are planning to conquer the universe?"

"No. We are too civilized for such paltry ambitions."

"All right. But you are propagating the hypno-beasts for some malign purpose. Revenge on another race?"

"No. We want the hypno-beasts killed as I told you. Every last one, if possible."

"But why then the bell jar experiment? There is some threat to my world. I feel it. You want Earth?"

"No. We do not wish your world, Earth!"

"Talk sense!" York groaned.

"Tony, don't ask wild questions and interrupt," Vera admonished. "Let him tell his story. Just listen."

Chapter 9

Vuldane nodded. "You would not have harmed me with your gun, by the way. This room is in an energy-less field. No weapon works in it. Now listen. This is the story of our race—and our doom!"

"We evolved to intelligence a million of your years ago. Vera and I have compared notes. We did not evolve under this sun, but under the rays of another Cepheid variable, at almost the other end of this universe. We lived there industriously and happily for a hundred thousand years. Then our astronomers announced that the sun was due soon to explode into a nova, killing all life on its planets. Cepheids are unstable stars.

"We had to migrate. But we had to find another Cepheid. And to make it difficult, we had to find a Cepheid with the exact period of waxing and waning that our original sun had—twenty-two days. Our biology, our metabolism, our very life-spark, is adjusted to that pulse beat, as yours is adjusted to a uniform condition."

"I think I understand," York said. "By analogy, on Earth, our most vigorous peoples are in the temperate zones, experiencing alternate winter and summer. Our tropical people are backward, and so are our Arctic people. We are adjusted to that variable pulse of life, though to you it would seem absolutely uniform. You, of course, are adjusted to a change from bitter cold to great heat, either of which would kill us."

"Clearly put," acknowledged Vuldane. "We found, after much searching, such a variable, and migrated to its planets. We set up our civilization and had another period of well being. Then that Cepheid reached the explosion point. Again we had to search for a twenty-two day Cepheid—one with planets, which are rare—and migrate to it. We have migrated a dozen times in the past million years, Anton York. We are nomads of the cosmos, never knowing a true home!" York felt the aura of sadness that suddenly radiated from the alien being. Certainly they were to be pitied for having been cursed to live under a temperamental star like a Cepheid, instead of a long-burning, stable sun, like Sol.

"We have been in this Cepheid system fifty thousand years," Vuldane resumed. "Two thousand years ago our astronomers again gave out their sickening omen. This sun would soon explode. Again the packing up, the elimination of all but a comparative few to start the race over, the departure from loved homes, deserted cities, the trials of rebuilding a new civilization. That faces us again."

"But why not migrate to a stable star and live under domes?" York objected. "You can duplicate any environment, as in the experiment domes. Surely you can duplicate your own."

"Live under domes?" The alien shook his head. "It would stultify the race, wither it away. It is not a good life. Would your Earth people like it?"

York thought back to Earth's colonization of the other planets. It was a tough existence. Young people aged rapidly. If Earth were to vanish, the remaining Earth race on other planets, in their sealed habitations, would die off through sheer strangulation.

"No, we must migrate to our type of sun," Vuldane stated. His thought-voice changed. "But this crisis is sharper than all others have been in the past. We have combed our universe from end to end. Only one twenty-two day Cepheid is left with a family of planets. The Cepheids of adjacent universes, like yours, are out of the question, for your astral laws are different. Our race would wither away as slowly but surely, in an alien universe, as under domes. We do not wish it. Thus that last Cepheid is our remaining hope. That is the last world possible for us! And now I come to that which affects your people—and the hypno-beasts."

He eyed York a moment, as though reluctant to go on. "That Cepheid has a family of ten planets, all inhabited by the hypno-beasts. Somehow their evolution inhibited them and they never became scientific. But they were endowed with the remarkable power of hypnotism. A kind of hypnotism to which our minds are peculiarly vulnerable. So strong did it seem that we doubted whether any minds could stand against it. But we had to find out.

"Thus we roamed our universe—and yours and others—and transplanted bits of inhabited worlds under the domes. We pitted them against the hypno-beasts. Our sole purpose was to find a race that could learn how to fight the Beasts, while using this universe's scientific laws."

The pieces all clicked into place abruptly in York's mind, with a stunning impact.

"I see," he murmured. "A colossal search for a race of creatures *parasitic* to the hypno-beasts! A race able to resist the hypnotism and *conquer* the Beasts!"

"In broad detail, just that," agreed Vuldane. "But for a long time we despaired of results. Most races succumbed to the hypnosis and became slaves of the hypno-beasts within a century or so. These we cast out as abortive cultures and procured new ones. In all, in the period of our long-range experiment, we have tried out more than ten thousand races, culled from seven universes!"

The staggering sweep of it overwhelmed York. Vera looked at him sympathetically. She had got over the first shock long before.

York looked at Vuldane, king of a driven, nomad race, in a new light. He and his people had the indomitable courage and never-say-die spirit that could only be admired in any race. York's thoughts leaped ahead.

"Earth people," he whispered. "Earth people are the ones!" Vuldane nodded, and somehow there was infinite regret in his manner.

"Yes, so it has proved. As with the many other races, we installed a thousand of your race in a dome, and pitted them against a control group of the hypno-beasts. One other remarkable, or damnable, attribute the hypno-beasts have. They are almost infinitely adaptable to any environment. They do not breathe oxygen. They absorb life energy from blood, any blood, and no extremes of temperature can stop them.

"We watched your race with avid interest for those two thousand years. We could not leap to conclusions. We used the true scientific method of thorough waiting. We watched as generation by generation your people developed immunity to the hypnotism. At the time you arrived, we had just about decided they were the ones. More, your rapid killing off of the hypno-beasts convinced us completely. Another race has developed immunity, but they do not have the scientific capabilities of yours."

York knew he was grinning in a ghastly, mirthless way. "You mean," he gasped, "that my coming decided you on my race, rather than the other? But I'm a special case. I'm an immortal among our race, and a super-scientist only because of that. You are overestimating—"

Vuldane smiled. "I cannot blame you for pleading in that way, trying to throw us off our decision. We know you are a special case. But you are still a sample of your race. The important thing is your race's capacity for science. We will furnish all the science necessary to destroy the hypno-beasts."

York pondered.

"You are supreme scientists. Why not simply ray down the beasts, with long-range beams from space, on their planets?"

"Do you think we haven't tried everything possible?" responded the alien. "We did that long ago. We rayed down all their centers and cities. We tried to cover every square inch of their planets. When we thought we had reduced their numbers to a safe minimum, we built fortresses. The inevitable happened. The Beasts rebred rapidly. They surrounded the fortresses in massed numbers, throwing their combined hypnosis within. Our people fell under the spell, were killed. The Beasts reigned again.

"You do not realize, Anton York, the tremendous power of their hypnosis in quantity. No minds in the universe can withstand it, except two. Those of your race and the non-scientific race."

"No diseases sowed among them could kill them off?" York queried. "No insect plagues them? Often it's the little things that conquer the big."

Again he got a withering smile.

"Before we used cultures of races, we gathered cultures of germs, worms, insects, crustaceans, plants. More than a million varieties of them. We sowed them among their planets. The hypno-beasts survived everything—everything. They are perhaps the most tenacious form of life in all the universe. Don't forget we have been trying for twenty centuries. No,

Anton York, only intelligence, immune to their hypnotism, will ever wipe them out."

York shrugged. "I must admit a certain degree of sympathy in your problem. I appoint myself emissary to my world, to tell them of your need for help. How many Earth people do you think you need?"

York saw the stricken look in Vera's eyes and prepared to hear a gigantic number.

"*All* of your people!" responded Vuldane softly.

York was past shock. He could only stare, as if turned to stone.

"All of your people," repeated the alien. "It will not be a simple task, even with Earth people immunity, and our science given to them. The time is short now, before our sun explodes. We must move all your people to the Beasts' planets, setting them up in fortresses which we will build. Many, perhaps most, of your people will succumb at first, till the following generations develop immunity. Finally they will wax strong, sweep out and conquer the Beasts completely. Then we will sow some disease among your people to kill *them,* and our new home will be ready for our occupancy."

York's psychic voice was a deadly hiss.

"By what right do you consider it your privilege to destroy my race to save yours?"

"By what right," returned Vuldane, "do you consider your race more worthy of continuation than mine? We were civilized long before yours. If you think we are merciless in sacrificing an alien race for our benefit, what of your own race? To this day it fights among itself at times. We haven't had internecine war for half a million years. Tell me, Anton York. Outside of your own personal prejudice, who is to judge whether we are wrong or right, except as necessity drives us?"

York could think of no answer. He knew now what Vera had meant before. It was the old story of Cro-magnon man killing off Neanderthal. White men destroying the redmen of America. Earth people expanding into interplanetary space and the flower people of Ganymede dying out. On a grander scale, this was the same thing. A vigorous, highly civilized, powerful race was grimly holding onto its place in the sun. Could they be blamed?

York answered at last. "No. There is no question of right or wrong in any scale of cosmic morals. But here is one thought, Vuldane. My people have millions of years ahead of them. Their sun is stable. You, on the other hand, are a doomed race. You will live another hundred thousand years in your new system, and then again that Cepheid will explode. Is it worth murdering my race, facing a million-year future, to save yours for one-tenth that? Can you pass into your inevitable oblivion with that on your conscience?"

"A strong point," nodded Vuldane. "Except for one thing. Our astronomers have measured all the stars. A new Cepheid is being born in a certain star group. It is beginning to pulse slowly. In the slow timescale of the cosmos, it will not be a full-fledged Cepheid for another hundred thousand years. But if we gain our new breathing spell, as outlined, that Cepheid will be ready for us. And other Cepheids are being born, our astronomers note. Through them, we also have a limitless future ahead of us!"

York deflated utterly. He could already picture, in his mind's eye, the nine planets of his sun, barren and deserted—human life gone. He looked up suddenly.

"All, you say, Vuldane. But there are more than ten billion of my race. Surely you can leave a few thousand behind, to breed our race again."

Vuldane shook his head, with a combination of pity and ruthlessness.

"No. We dare not leave any of your race. Once they grew strong again, we would only have to destroy them later. Better that your race goes into total oblivion now."

York could see that point, too. Knowing the crusade spirit of his own people, they would one day swoop down on the Korians, to right an old wrong. There would only be bitter interstellar war. The Korians, for their own sake, would have to guard against that.

And again it was not a question of right or wrong, or cruelty, or anything in normal terms. This was something above and beyond such meaningless phrases out of Earth's old law books.

"How much time is there?" he asked dully. "How soon before your Cepheid explodes into a nova?"

"Just a short thousand years. It will take all that time to bring your people, set them all in fortresses, and help them battle the beasts. And for us to migrate, when that is done. The time is short."

York drew himself up.

"Only one thing I ask, Vuldane."

"Yes?"

"Before you begin taking my people, give me a certain time to try to figure out some alternative."

Vuldane pondered. "The transference should begin immediately. However, it will take a year to complete our first fleet of ships capable of plunging through the space-time wall that separates our two universes. I give you that year, Anton York."

Suddenly he thrust out his spindly hand.

"And good luck!"

Chapter 10

York's ship sped through the void at a pace that left laggard light far behind. His face was grimly set as he took a course for the planetary system of the hypno-beasts. Vuldane had readily given the data.

"A year, Vera," York said desolately. "A short year in which to save the human race! I must not sleep for that year. Drugs will keep me going. Somehow there must be a way."

"What do you expect to do among the Beasts?" Vera asked tonelessly.

"Anything," York stated. "Anything possible."

In a day they were there. The Cepheid sun was an exact duplicate of the one they had left. Its ten planets were large and widespread, fairly crawling with the hateful hypno-beasts. They had a semi-civilization. They bred whole races of creatures for their blood-food, for their ten planets of loathsome vampirism. Luckily they had no space ships. The whole universe— this and all others—would become theirs. They populated the ten planets simply through the accident of separate, parallel development.

York could feel the powerful beat of their hypnotic force radiating en masse from them. It dragged at his mind as gravity dragged at his ship. Recklessly he power-dived over one planet, spraying down his gamma-sonic rays, cutting a wide swath among them. The hypno-force clutched at him. Twice more he dived recklessly, and barely won free the third time.

"Tony, please! It's senseless."

York nodded helplessly.

"I need a long-range projector. We'll build one. No. We'll have the Korians build us one."

The ship sped back the way it had come. Vuldane readily agreed. Almost overnight his technicians turned out a super-projector for York's ship and back he raced. With this he whipped his ship in a right orbit around one planet and sprayed down the destroying rays in a band ten miles wide, from directly above the surface.

"If this works, Vera," he said in vague hope, "we'll have a million more made. And I'll go to Earth and get a million strong-minded men, and we'll sweep every planet clean. The Korians weren't able to get close enough to the planet."

But gradually he felt the finger of hypnotic force reach for him. His telescope revealed thousands of the massed hypno-beasts below, directing a combined hypno-ray upward at him. He kept up his deadly beam even when he felt the cloying, insidious urge to drop down and yield to the Beasts. Sweat beaded his brow. God, what frightful mental power they had!

He had not watched Vera. Suddenly he noticed her at the locked controls, unhitching them and plunging the ship down. Her movements were jerky, robotlike. She was in a hypnotized trance.

"Vera!"

York left his gun and leaped for her. She turned on him, clawing and scratching. York bit his lip and swung his fist, knocking her cold. He zoomed the ship up, barely in time. His whole body had begun stiffening at the powerful clutch of massed hypnotism from below. He whipped the ship into free space.

"Vera, forgive me," he muttered when he brought her to with a dash of cold water. "Well, that's out. The men from Earth would have as little, or less chance than I had."

"Vuldane said they tried everything," Vera murmured hopelessly. "Theirs is the only way. Setting Earth people down there, after blasting a space with their super-science. Letting them breed and produce immune generations. A thousand-year job, Tony—and we have only a year. It might as well be a second."

York did not give up. He thought next of a screen against the hypnotic force. Back at the Korian world, he consulted with Vuldane.

"There is no screen against their hypnosis," Vuldane stated flatly. "We have tried. You noticed that your mental telepathy barely worked through our energy wall. Yet that energy wall is absolutely transparent to their hypnotic force!"

"Still, I want to try," ground out York desperately. "I must. Give me one dome as a proving ground, and all the materials I need."

"Agreed," nodded Vuldane quickly. "I sympathize with you, York. But I have no hope for you."

York tried everything in the next few months. He had a group of chained hypno-beasts as control, and set before them shields of various composition. Metal alloys, plastics, radium-coated diamond, and then more subtle walls of electro-magnetic energy, cosmic rays, even a vacuum. In each case, stationing himself with the shield between, their hypnotic force came through undiminished.

Vuldane was right. There was no shield to that demonic mental vibration.

"Tony, please, you must rest," Vera insisted as he staggered and would have fallen except for her arm. "You haven't closed your eyes in months."

But York went on, sleepless, taxing the superb vitality of his immortal body to the utmost.

"There must be a way," he chanted steadily, as though he were a child reciting a poem.

Vuldane came to visit him at times, and even made suggestions. Admiration for York shone from his alien eyes.

"If anything at all can make me feel a pang of regret over sacrificing your race, it is you, Anton York. A race that produces such as you deserves continuation." Then, in the next breath he added: "But my race must continue!"

"Vuldane, did you try everything?" York pleaded. "Did you try creating planetary earthquakes, floods, volcanic eruptions?"

The Korian nodded. "Naturally. We nearly disrupted one planet entirely, instituting a planet-wide geological upheaval. For a century the planet seemed clear. Not one hypno-beast appeared. Then suddenly they cropped up again from somewhere."

"An atomic fire, sweeping the whole planet's surface?" cried York. "How about that?"

"And how would you stop the atomic fire from eating inward, consuming the entire planet to ash?"

"The hypnosis itself," sighed York. "That's the angle I must work from. We can't resist it or shield it. But how about a neutralizing projector?"

Fired with the new idea, York built what was essentially a scrambler, or a device that would spray out static to the hypnotic force. He was able to cast a field around his dozen control beasts and break up their flow of hypnosis into intermittent flashes. Borrowing a super-powerful generator from the Korians, York raced to the other Cepheid.

With the static machine going full blast, he was able to land on one planet. Hypno-beasts began crowding around this invasion of their world.

York sprayed his static around, neutralizing their hypno-force. Then he swept his gun in a circle, whiffing out the monsters like a row of lighted candles.

It was as though he had touched off a hidden spring. A signal must have gone around the planet. Over the horizon marched incredible droves of them. They massed around the ship in such numbers that York's lethal ray was like a little machinegun against all the armies of Alexander, Caesar and Napoleon combined. Sheer weight of numbers would win out.

"Tony, they're getting nearer—"

"Yes, but if we had a million scramblers and a million guns, it would work!" York shouted happily. "Simple mathematics."

And then it happened. With a tortured grind, the static machine sputtered and died. Like a tidal wave, the full force of hypnotism struck them, no longer scrambled. Vera passed instantly into a trance. York, with an effort of will that seemed to tear his brain up by the roots, jerked over the engine lever. The ship darted upward at a pace that took them out of the hypnotic range in seconds.

"Just in time," York muttered. He looked over his static machine thoughtfully, incredulously. It was a fused mass! When they were back, Vuldane explained.

"We tried that too. The hypno-beasts are canny. Their technique is simple. They pour a massed hypno-force at the scrambler, overload it, and burn it out. We tried generators with world-moving power. They burned them all out. When will you begin to realize, Anton York, that this is a thousand-year job? We've planned it as such. It is not something that you can toss off overnight."

York looked stricken.

"I'm sorry," said Vuldane simply and sincerely, before leaving.

York looked at Vera. Not a shred of hope remained.

"Think of it, Vera," he said hollowly. "Our race was doomed as far back as the nineteenth century, when the Korians came to take an Earth culture back with them. Even before you and I were born, our people were doomed unknowingly. I destroyed fifty Immortals, and Mason Chard, and fought the Three Eternals, to save civilization. I was even ready to sacrifice myself. And all the time, another race in another universe had put their finger on us and marked us for oblivion. Our whole life and effort, all my superscience and guidance of Earth, has been a mockery, a cosmic joke, a jest of the gods."

Vera soothed him in ways she had learned through two thousand years of association. His weary head sought refuge in her lap. His bloodshot eyes closed for the first time in six months.

"All mockery," he said bitterly. "I've had the thought of going back to Earth and destroying it, so that oblivion for them will be quicker and more merciful. Lighting an atomic fire on all the planets— It would be swift."

"No, Tony. That would be pure spite against the Korians. Whatever they've been forced to do, they are a highly civilized, deserving race."

"Fire!" York jerked erect, repeating his own word. A dawning look came over his face. "Fighting fire with fire! Vera, maybe that's the answer. Instead of fighting them with our weapons, why not fight them with theirs?"

Sleep forgotten, hope reborn, York became twice the dynamo of activity he had been before.

"Time is short—six months. I have to measure the wavelength of the hypno-force, and then duplicate it."

Six months. Six months in which York explored the psycho-magnetic scale. Earth's scientists had taken two centuries to piece out the electro-magnetic scale. York condensed the same amount of research into a six-month snap of the fingers.

In the electro-magnetic scale were the octaves of radio waves, infra-red, visible light, ultra-violet, X-rays, gamma rays and cosmic rays.

In the psycho-magnetic range, York found the octaves of telepathy, clairvoyance, sixth-sense, hunch, hallucination, dreams. Far down the scale, like the elusive cosmic rays, he found the hypnotic range.

These super-penetrative radiations of hypnotism he measured with all the accuracy of an astro-physicist studying a spectrograph. They were so incredibly fine that York hazily understood them to slip through the interstices of the ether itself, as cosmic rays slipped through the planetary atoms.

"Now I know exactly what the hypno-source is," York stated. "Vuldane, did you try to build a projector?" For the first time, Vuldane shook his head. "This is a great achievement, York. But I'm afraid you can't build a projector. Not a mechanical one. Evolution produced the projector—an organic brain—after millions of years. You won't duplicate that in the time left, even the full thousand years."

York saw the logic of it. Then a strange look came into his eye.

"No. But I already have the projector." He tapped his own forehead. "All I have to do is find the way to increase its powers to equal the brain projectors of the hypno-beasts!"

"Good luck," said Vuldane again.

His sympathetic smile, as he left, told of no hope for the outcome.

Precious time slipped by.

York worked entirely from the biological angle. With a super X-ray, he went minutely over the brain of one of the captive hypno-beasts, studying its cells, analyzing it completely. When at last he had the answer, he had withdrawn a precious hormone from it. But would it work?

Vera volunteered to be the guinea pig. Anton looked at her for a long moment. "It might mean death," he said grimly.

Vera was adamant, and Anton relented. He injected a few drops of the new hormone into the base of Vera's neck, and watched for the results with eyes that burned with hope and dread. Vera went into a coma. Her skin became cold. Her heart stopped. York stood quietly, fighting for control.

An hour later, death drew back. Vera's super-vitality rallied and life returned. She sat up, smiling. York said nothing. Words meant nothing now. Silently he led her to the test chamber, before a group of starved hypno-beasts. He locked her in. They surrounded her, eyeing her and closing in. Vera went rigid. Their eager tentacles stretched for her soft white neck.

York turned away, shuddering. Failure, after all!

Suddenly, within the chamber, the situation changed. As though an invisible blast had blown them back, the hypno-beasts fell away from Vera.

She stood up, her eyes blazing. One by one the Beasts rolled over and went rigid, in complete hypnosis.

Vuldane, when they faced him, was skeptical.

"I can't do anything about it, York. I can't recall the ships sent to bring the first of your people. We have little time as it is to start our grand plan. I can't take a chance on your hypothetical anti-hypnosis hormone."

"Make this test," York demanded. "Send a shipful of your men to the Beast system, after they have been given my hormone injection. Command them to land among the thickest of the Beast communities and stay for ten hours. If they don't come back, I won't be able to fight your plan."

Vuldane agreed. York injected the men, rescuing them from the death-like effects by heroic doses of drugs. The ship left.

Waiting for its return was a refinement of torture that ground York's nerves to shreds. The hours stumbled by like his entire lifetime.

"Tony—look!"

The ship appeared. The Korians leaped out, eagerly telling their story of withstanding mass hypnotism for ten hours, and hypnotizing a ring of Beasts in turn.

Vuldane turned to York.

"You have saved your people, Anton York. It is a monumental achievement. I will recall the first fleet immediately. All the culture races will be returned to their worlds. I cannot express my joy and relief that we are not forced to sacrifice your race. You may go back to your people now, and tell them they are saved."

York shook his head. A strange look rested in his eyes, for this was the strangest thing of all the past episode.

"No. It is a story they would hardly believe. The only evidence for it would be the vanishing of a thousand people from Fort Mojave in eighteen-eighty-eight. That trifling event has long been forgotten and most likely unrecorded. Humanity was saved without knowing it was doomed. That will have to remain my secret."

Vera nodded. It was a chapter of the mythology of Anton York that would never be written for the eyes of the Earth. It was the secret of Anton York.

Epilogue

Back on Earth, before the two colossi of diamond on Mount Everest, the yearly commemoration ceremony paeaned to its sad denouement.

"Anton York, benefactor of humanity, is dead!"